Blood Ties

outskirts
press

Outskirts Press, Inc.
http://www.outskirtspress.com

ISBN: 978-1-9772-0287-1

Cover Image by Tess Adaoag

Outskirts Press and the "OP" logo are trademarks belonging to Outskirts Press, Inc.

PRINTED IN THE UNITED STATES OF AMERICA

To:

*My friends and family who wouldn't stop giving
me grief until I finished writing this book*

T. W. Kirchner who edited and proofread

And Patrick Appnel who sponsored my publishing

Chapter 1
Arizu

My father had just nudged me as I slept in the car, yet in an instant I was already fully awake and hyper.

"Are we finally there?" I looked at him excitedly as he turned the car off.

"We are. Are you ready, Arizu?"

"Of course! Let's go!" I grabbed my cap from where I had thrown it onto the back seat and jumped out of my dad's Jeep. I pulled it on quickly to hide my very weird and unexplainable ears.

They were blonde – the same color as my hair – fuzzy, and were the ears of a dingo. Plus, they were up on *top* of my head. That would be weird to any human in and of itself. I also wore my thick hair long and down to cover the absence of human ears.

My father and I walked up the driveway of the little house we were parked in front of and knocked on the worn door. A tall, older man with thin, graying hair named Jaspes greeted us.

"Hey, Grandpa!" I said happily as I gave him a hug. I

then hurried past him into the little house, making way for my dad to enter as well. My father gave a short greeting to Jaspes and then followed me in. Grandpa Jaspes closed the door behind him.

The little house wasn't much to describe. Just a single-story, two bedroom, one bathroom house. A little living room sat to the left of the entry and a small kitchen sat to the right, and a hallway facing the door led to the rest of the rooms. For right now, I headed to the bathroom.

When I returned, a slightly hunched over woman with completely gray hair was now present.

"Hi, Grandma Paryle!" I gave her a hug, love spreading through me at being able to see my grandparents again.

Paryle was Grandpa's second marriage on my mother's side of the family tree, but I loved her just as much as I would if she were my blood relative. Together, my grandma and grandpa were some of the kindest, nicest, most loving, and most caring people EVER!

When we separated, I marveled once again at how fast Grandma's hair had turned gray. It had still been amber colored only last year.

"Your hair still always fascinates me!" I said to her.

She gave a chuckle and replied, "Well, when you've lived here on Earth for so long, your hair is sure to lose its color."

Grandma and Grandpa were actually quite a few years older than they looked. They could pass for around three-fourths their actual age. This was only possible because they were former Lyvens.

Lyvens were, in short, lycanthropes; people who could change from a human form into an animal form. The most common type of lycanthrope in Earth lore was a werewolf. Though that certainly wasn't the only type of lycanthrope, humans didn't know Lyvens existed. So, you couldn't really blame them for getting their facts wrong.

Lyvens lived on a completely different planet than Earth, a planet called Cillium. Time worked differently on the bodies of its inhabitants. It's not that Lyvens lived longer than humans, but actually that they're bodies aged slower after hitting a certain age. It depended on the Lyven, but the most common age for this to happen was twenty. So Lyvens would have lived eighty years but still looked as if they were in their fifties.

Lyvens normally couldn't have lived for more than a month on Earth, but my grandpa and grandma had volunteered to live their lives as humans. They were stripped of all Lyven abilities in order to survive on Earth to watch over a Gate. This Gate linked the world of the Lyvens to Earth. The reason behind their decision was to keep our family together. For my mother had somehow met and fallen in love with my father, a human.

This was a mystery and a story my father never told me. Humans had no idea about our existence. In fact, my dad was the only human to know.

After giving birth to me, I was told that my mother died from an exponential amount of blood loss. Because of this, my grandparents unselfishly gave up their Lyven abilities in order to guard the Gate from being destroyed by our species, allowing me the opportunity to stay with my only living parent and still be able to visit my other half's kind. I would forever be grateful to them, for my cousin (and best friend), lived on Cillium.

"Ready for lunch?" my grandma asked, snapping me back to the present.

"You betcha!" I replied, hopping from one foot to another. Once lunch was over, I would head through the Gate to get to Cillium. And I could hardly wait!

Knowing my obvious canine side, Grandpa had cooked steak, and Grandma had made beef stew with fresh baked rolls. My favorite type of fruit, peaches, was also served.

Unlike most canines, dingoes also ate fruit, and I was no exception.

Light conversation was made, though mostly between either my grandparents and I or my father and I. The three of them didn't really get along, but they tried their hardest to do so for my sake, and I was thankful for that.

After lunch was finished and all of us pitched in to clean up, I hugged my family good-bye and headed toward the second, unoccupied bedroom where the Gate was located. Stepping inside the room, I closed the door behind me. Because I visited Cillium so often, I practically lived there as well and had no need to bring anything from this world over. Well, besides me, of course.

I looked with half-shut eyes at the blindingly brilliant light of the Gate. It was impossible to describe what it looked like exactly, for the light around it always seemed to be moving and changing shape. It was quite disorienting.

Walking up to the Gate, I unlocked the mechanism that kept it shut, and went through. As always, a strange, yet warm and familiar feeling enveloped me as I passed through to Cillium. Soon, I was standing on the other side of the

Gate. I locked the mechanism back up and then took in my surroundings.

I was in a small back room of my cousin's mansion. It was more like a utility closet than anything, especially when compared to the grand rooms of the rest of the place. I quickly ducked out of the room and started traversing the beautiful marble corridors.

My cousin's mom and dad weren't the type to show their power by flaunting exquisite art or neat knick-knacks. They showed their power through intimidation. This was displayed in the form of muted black and gray accents that wove throughout the hallways – standing as a stark contrast to the white of the marble.

I wasn't interested in any of the intimidation tactics, though. I had walked these halls countless times before, and they didn't even make me bat an eye anymore. No, the only thing I was interested in doing was seeing my cousin. And maybe *finally* getting a scare on her.

I knew where and how to avoid all the cameras placed throughout the mansion, and I knew the places where my cousin spent most of her time. Even without setting off any alarms, she wouldn't be easy to scare. She had nerves of steel, and it bothered me so badly that her special ability was seeing a single deep fear a Lyven had. Because of her ability, she scared me so often with what I feared. What that was, exactly, doesn't need to be shared.

Since Lyvens were animal hybrids, they could shape-shift into their specific animals whenever they wanted. But along with that, every Lyven had one other specific special ability, and every single ability was different. Well, except for me.

I could usually shape-shift no problem, unless I was under immense pressure, but I didn't have an ability of my own. The reason behind this was most likely caused by my human inheritance, but that was okay! It didn't bother me anymore.

I now finally approached my cousin's room, the best place to find her. I stayed low and hugged the walls, still undetected. The door was shut but most likely unlocked, even if she was out somewhere else. I gently grabbed the handle, turned it slowly, and burst through the doorway with what resembled a war cry. What greeted me was...

"Nice try, idiot." Roxlin was sitting in her swiveling desk chair facing the door that I had just come barging through.

"How did you know?" I complained, though not really surprised. Roxlin always gave me a different answer for how she could tell I was coming, though, so I asked anyways. The new information helped me with trying to figure out a perfect strategy to scare her.

"Well when you come marching up to my door like an elephant, I'm sure to feel the vibrations of your footfalls. I'm a Snake Lyven, remember?"

"Yeah, yeah. You remind me of that every time! So not fair." I went and pulled my cousin from her chair to give her a hug. She hated physical contact, so I hugged her just to bother her.

"Alright enough, you smelly dog. Get off me." I pulled away from Roxlin and gave her my trademark cheesy smile. I then proceeded to take my cap off and threw it onto her bed. It always felt so much better not to have to smash my ears down. Not to mention I could hear a whole lot better without the cap on!

"It's been a couple months! How are you and what have you been up to?" I asked my cousin. Roxlin looked at me with her round, black, unblinking eyes. Unlike popular belief on Earth, most snakes that hunted during the day had circular pupils instead of the vertically slit ones. And Roxlin, being a Coluber constrictor hybrid, was a daytime hunter.

"I'm good, and not much. I just got done slaughtering a bunch of people in my game on my PC."

"I thought you only played that one life simulation game that isn't even violent on your PC."

"Yeah. So?" I blinked slowly at Roxlin.

"Well let's go do something fun! Let's go to the park!"

"But I don't wanna leave my room," Roxlin complained.

"Just think though. You can get ice cream from Ulon's Ice Cream if you come with me!" I wriggled my eyebrows up and down at her.

After a pause, she replied, "Fine. But if you touch my ice cream like last time, I'll bite one of your ears off, okay?"

"Okay!"

"Freaking mutt." I laughed and bounded out the door and down the hallway, Roxlin following more slowly behind.

On our way to the front door, we passed one of the housekeepers that worked in Roxlin's house. She had been there for a long time, and I knew her well.

"Hi Sou!" I called to her as I skipped along.

"Well, this is a pleasant surprise," she responded with a wave. "Where are you off to so quickly, Arizu?"

"I'm off to the park with Roxlin!" I replied.

"Oh my. I think this is the first time the young Master has been out in three weeks! You always were good for her." Roxlin trudged by and the Bear Lyven turned to address her. "You really should get some fresh air more often, young Master."

"Hmph," was her only response.

"Come on. Hurry, Roxlin!" We had finally made it to the massive front door of my cousin's mansion. I waited impatiently with my hand tapping on the door handle.

"What for? We still have plenty of time before the sun sets."

"I know, but I finally get to walk around without having to worry about being found out as a Lyven! You have no idea how hard it is to always have to pretend to be an average human. I can't do anything fun for fear of my ears being noticed."

"You have such a hard life," Roxlin said flatly. She caught up, brushed my hand aside, and opened the door to the outside.

Cillium was beautiful. Don't get me wrong. Earth was, too. But Cillium had an ethereal beauty. I didn't go to school here so I didn't know much about the science of the planet, but something about the magic that was in Cillium's atmosphere turned the sky pink when its sun rose. At night, the sky turned to a deep, dark purple.

Because of the pink sky during the day, everything was tinted that color. It made everything seem. . . happier. More peaceful. Other than that and the inhabitants, Cillium wasn't much different than Earth. The trees, green grass, mountain ranges, work places, and animals were but a few similarities. Only the society seemed vastly different.

There was still a high-class, middle-class, and lower-class among the Lyvens, but it wasn't based on money. Maybe it was the animal side of all Lyvens that made us laugh at the prospect of needing money to give the incentive of making a living. No, the Lyvens based class off of how powerful one was. If you stood up for yourself and could actually defend the position you had taken, your peers backed off and respected that. There was always the prospect of being knocked down by a new challenger, but nowadays, most Lyvens were content with their lifestyles. The only bad thing about being in the Lower-Class was not having as many rights as the classes above. But the discrimination wasn't so bad nowadays either. Well, in most cases.

Roxlin and I had just barely made it to the park when an annoyingly high-pitched voice rang out.

"Oh, look who came to visit. It's the *half-blood dweeb* and her *guard snake*. I'm surprised the Snake is even alive, seeing as how long it's been since she came out of her hole." Avo was a Cat Lyven. And a giant pain to deal with. My ears flattened back at hearing Avo, and I couldn't hold back a growl of annoyance. It usually took a lot to get me worked up, but just seeing Avo's face and hearing her voice set me on edge. I wasn't all that great at comebacks, but oh boy was Roxlin good at it.

"Don't you have a dumpster that you need to go dive in?" she taunted Avo in a scalding tone. "Trash like you should be around its own kind." Fury built up in Avo's face, and it made me smile.

My ears pricked back up and I quickly said, "It really has been a pleasure to see you once again, *friend*." I used my fingers and mimed quotation marks around *friend*. "But my cousin and I have places to be. Bye!" I grabbed Roxlin's wrist and sprinted with her to the small ice cream shop that rested on the other side of the park. Once inside, I busted out laughing.

"I think that was your best comeback yet!" I sputtered out between gasps of breath.

Roxlin was giving her rare, fanged grin and even chuckled. "Well, I was just stating the obvious."

"Ain't that the truth!" I laughed. After calming down somewhat, my cousin and I ordered some ice cream. Straight chocolate for me, and cookies n' cream for Roxlin. Once finished, we went outside to hang out for the rest of the day. Luckily, Avo was nowhere to be seen.

It didn't matter that I'd turned sixteen five months ago, because the dingo blood running through me was mostly the cause of me usually always acting like a six-year-old. And playing hide-and-go-seek was one of my favorite games! Though she complained about it, Roxlin always humored me and played along. Maybe she did so because I would play video games with her, or maybe because she was technically my guardian while I was on Cillium. It could also be out of a sense of family duty. But I liked to think that it was because, even with all her grumbling and complaining, she loved the game just as much as I did. And our competitions were epic.

Though I had trouble switching between my animal form and my humanoid form at times, I could usually do so if I concentrated hard enough and didn't feel too pressured. Which was good for me because switching from humanoid to animal form gave many different benefits and weaknesses to both of Roxlin and I. Thanks to that, our games usually ended with a tie. We both hated to lose anyway, so it worked out.

The sun had just settled behind the mountains to the west when we finished our last game.

"Those were such good matches once again!" I said in contentment.

Roxlin had a small smile on her face as we sat on the grass watching the purple hue take over from the pink. She pushed a strand of her long black hair from out of her face. "It was."

"Hey, let's get some more ice cream before we go home!" I suggested. I clasped my hands together in a pleading gesture and stared at Roxlin with a hopeful gaze.

"No way," she said dismissively. "We'll be having dinner soon and you'll ruin your appetite if you do." I stared at Roxlin for a moment. My cousin shook her head. "Ah, right. I sometimes forget that your stomach is a bottomless pit. Fine. Let's go. But you're gonna have to eat it while walking home. I don't want to be late for dinner. I'm hungry."

"Alrighty!" Together, we got up and walked to Ulon's Ice Cream. I was so looking forward to another bowl of my favorite ice cream! But my stomach dropped when I saw who loitered around the interior of the shop.

"Twice in one day! *How lucky.*" Avo leaned against the red wall to the left of the shop entrance, looking cocky. She now had her friends with her.

Chapter 2
Roxlin

Irritation bubbled beneath my skin. There was only so much stupidity I could take in one day. I really hoped that Arizu and I could quickly make a break for it and slip through the door, but two of Avo's lackies had already blocked our exit. I sighed in exasperation. I had just spent the rest of the day playing games with my hyper cousin and was exhausted. I *really* didn't want to have to deal with Avo again. But, unfortunately, it seemed we would have to.

"Seeing you once today was already torture enough. Do we really have to deal with you again *and* your gang of prepubescent losers?" I rubbed my temples in annoyance. A snort of laughter escaped from Arizu at my insults. I could see that I had riled the five bullies up because they all shifted threateningly.

I glanced at the shop counter, but no one was there. Avo must have noticed this, for she grinned at me.

"He's gone to the bathroom. You can't get help from any adults now. How about we take you outside and teach you a lesson in manners? Maybe then you won't go spouting off your mouth so much during our next encounter."

I raised an eyebrow. "I'd love to, but there seems to be two of your henchmen blocking the exit."

Avo smoothed down her brown hair as her blue eyes flashed menacingly. "An easy fix."

"Sure it is. But you've always been too scared to do anything physical to me because of my parents. Why so bold now?"

Avo huffed proudly. "My parents just worked their way into a higher position in this city. Your parents can't do anything to me now." With that, she waved the two kids standing next to her forward to grab Arizu and me.

I felt the vibrations from the footfalls of the two behind us as. The air swished by as the one behind me moved quickly to grab me.

These kids had made a big mistake.

I crouched slightly and gripped his arm as it went through the spot my shoulder had just been. I then proceeded to use his momentum to throw him over my back, and he landed with a gratifying *thump* onto a table in front of me. I glanced over to see if Arizu was alright even as I kicked out at my next attacker. My foot caught her on the side of her head and she went down. I smiled to myself when I saw my cousin using the self-defense techniques I had taught her against her own assailants.

With Arizu having quickly immobilized her two attackers as well, I now turned my attention to Avo. Shock filled her gaze and she backed away from Arizu and I. I could see sweat form across her brow. She had clearly not expected to have her friends be taken down, especially not so quickly.

I had forced Arizu to learn self-defense techniques from

me after she had come home one night from a walk with a purple face and broken hand. Even without knowing how to fight, she had apparently punched a kid in the face so hard it had shattered two knuckles. And I was so glad she had been able to hold her own tonight. The look on Avo's face was priceless.

"Um, well, here, look," Avo grasped desperately for words. "I wasn't really going to try to hurt either of you. It was all just a prank! Yeah! And. . . and. . ."

I stalked toward the Cat Lyven. I had always known that she was behind all the times Arizu came back from somewhere with wounds across her body, but I hadn't had any proof. Arizu being half human, basically everyone treated her as talking garbage and wouldn't have ever believed her word over Avo's even if she had spoken up in her own defense. But this time. . . Oh man, Avo had messed up. She'd not attacked me, but she'd had the gall to attack my cousin in front of me. Even with her parents' new positions, my parents had been High-Class for a lot longer than hers. My word was worth more.

I stopped in front of Avo, and she cowered before me. I grabbed her neck and yanked her face up within inches of mine. I bared my fangs. "All my life I've had to eat substitute meat to sate my hunger. I wonder how real meat tastes?" Just then, the bell on the glass door of Ulon's Ice Cream jingled. A flicker of alarm shot through me and I quickly looked over my shoulder to see who it was. Luckily, it was just a solitary kid who seemed around the same age as the rest of us.

He gaped at the unconscious and groaning Lyvens before his gaze landed on me. Scales that ran across his forehead and flowed partly down the left side of his face indicated he was either an Alligator or Crocodile Lyven. Mind you, I was in a very awkward and incriminating pose – with my hand around someone's throat and all. Thankfully, Arizu stepped up to the kid and began talking to him, probably trying to explain what was going on.

I turned my attention back to Avo. Thanks to my ability to know one of her deepest fears, I could see that one of the Cat Lyven's fears was heights. I bared my fangs again, but now in a smile. "Seems you've been saved by the bell. However, if you ever try to attack either one of us again, not only will I get my parents involved, I will personally drop you off the tallest building in this city. Understood?"

Whether from my words or because of my black, unsettling, unblinking eyes, her trembling body gave away that she was completely terrified. She nodded quickly, and I released her throat. She stumbled away from me, grabbing onto a chair to help steady herself. I looked back to where Arizu was still talking to the new kid and headed over to them.

"Yeah, so no need to tell anyone about this, alright?" Arizu had apparently just finished her explanation. The kid gazed at her with his yellowish-green eyes. He shrugged and said,

"Sure. I used to get into fights with the kids in my previous neighborhood all the time, so you don't need to worry about me telling anyone." The kid seemed nonchalant about the whole situation, but even so, I wanted to make sure I had leverage just in case. I used my ability on him and saw that one of his deepest fears was... Spiders? A boy who was obviously trying to seem cool with his baggy T-shirt, cargo pants, sunglasses resting atop dark brown hair, and a single piercing in his left ear, was scared of spiders?

I stared at him for a moment before taking Arizu by the arm. I guided her toward the door, but she resisted. "Wait but my ice cream?" Arizu asked with a pouting look on her face.

"You got some earlier. After all this, it's best to just head home," I told her. Arizu looked grumpy about the whole situation, and she stuck her tongue out at Avo before letting me lead her to the door. Right before going through, though, the Alligator/Crocodile Lyven stopped us.

"Hey, wait! I, uh, I'm actually new here and don't know anyone. I'm Kaylon. You guys are?"

I saw Arizu perk up at the prospect of a friend. "I'm Arizu!" she said excitedly.

I stayed quiet, contemplating if this kid had an ulterior motive for being friendly. Although he was new, he had to know of my family. My family of Coluber constrictor snakes had been in the high-class for a long time and was well-known. If this kid, Kaylon, was trying to be friendly only to get into good graces with my family to further himself, I wouldn't play along.

Unfortunately, though, my cousin trusted people way too easily. She elbowed me because I stayed silent. "Rox, introduce yourself!"

I sighed. "I'm Roxlin. Now, I dislike fake people, so we'll be going now." I turned toward the door.

"Who said I was fake?" Kaylon asked with humor coating his voice.

I sighed again and turned back to him. "No one did. It was an assumption based on my thought process. Would you like me to fix my sentence? Fine. I dislike most people, and you are included in that group. Therefore, Arizu and I will be going now." Amusement flashed in Kaylon's yellowish-green eyes, and he gave a toothy grin. "Well, alright then. But I hope I'll see you two around again sometime."

Arizu's smile couldn't get any wider. She seemed just about to burst with joy. I rolled my eyes at her happiness, but internally felt a tug of sympathy for the half-Lyven. She had made the mistake of telling her heritage to Avo when she had first visited the city of Avera. Avo had immediately told everyone she could, and rumors spread like wildfire. After that, Arizu was treated no better than dirt. So Kaylon saying that he hoped to see her again must have brought her so much joy.

"You don't want to be friends with those two," an angry voice said. "Especially the mistake called a 'half-Lyven.'" We all turned to see the boy I had thrown onto a table get shakily to his feet. Avo was still where I had left her, warily watching and waiting for us to leave. "That one-," he pointed at Arizu. "That one has a *human father.*" I looked at Arizu's ashen face, despair at the prospect of being shunned by another Lyven sweeping over her. Kaylon stood impassively, and I couldn't read his expression. But before anything else could be said, I was in front of the boy in an instant. How *dare* he ruin my cousin's chance at another friend after only having me in this world for so long?

"You shouldn't have said that," I hissed. I grabbed his arm, spun him around, twisted it behind his back, and pushed up with all my strength. A satisfying *snap* sounded, and the boy cried out in pain.

"Next time," I told him, "you should remember to keep your mouth closed." I released him. He whimpered and fell to the ground, cradling his arm. "Anyone else want to say anything?" I looked around the room at the rest of Avo's group. The ones not knocked out shook their heads hastily. "Good. None of this leaves this room, then. If any of you think to use this against my family, I promise that there will be serious backlash. Tell that to your friends when they wake up." Just then, the worker tending Ulon's Ice Cream finally came back from his bathroom break. He took in the cowering teenagers and looked at me questioningly.

"A minor argument," I waved dismissively. Without waiting for a response, I marched to where my cousin was standing next to Kaylon, grabbed her arm, and finally got her out of the shop. Arizu gave a regretful look behind us at Ulon's Ice Cream, but followed obediently behind me nonetheless.

"If Kaylon decides not to be friends with you just because of your heritage, then he wasn't someone worth your time, alright?" I told her gruffly. She nodded absentmindedly. I continued leading her on, worried about her mental health.

When all the bad rumors about Arizu began circulating, my parents had contemplated throwing her out. However, due to my dad being Arizu's late mother's brother, he just didn't have the heart to. But the bullying was one reason why she never came to Avera during the school year. Arizu had said many times before that she preferred going to school on Earth. She still knew a lot about Cillium from me, though. I liked to teach her things so that she wouldn't be completely left out. However, dingoes were social animals, and though she had never said so, I had pieced together from what she had occasionally let slip that she was an outcast on Earth as well. It wasn't good for her to only have me to rely on here and only have her father and grandparents to be with on Earth.

Since the park was only a few minute's walk from my house, we arrived there shortly and went inside. The smell of the substitute meat carnivores were provided filled the entryway. We followed the smell to the kitchen.

The kitchen inside my parents' house was large. It had all the bells and whistles, though me not liking to cook, I had no idea what half the stuff was called. Sou was there, an apron on and a large knife in her hand.

"Hello, girls!" She called when she spotted us. Arizu bounced happily up to probably the only other Lyven besides me that didn't treat her like garbage. Maybe it was because she was a fellow canine, but that didn't seem like the case. Whatever the reason, I was grateful. I saw looks of disgust pass between the other kitchen workers, but one glare from me sent them back to focusing on their preparations for dinner.

"What are you making for dinner tonight?" my cousin asked.

The Bear Lyven smiled. "Well, I didn't have time to make your favorite meal since you came so suddenly, but I did whip up some pork chops for tonight. What do you think?"

Arizu bounced up and down alongside Sou and I. "That's my second favorite meal! Thank you!" Sou laughed and I gave a small smile. There was something about Arizu's happiness that was contagious. How Lyvens wouldn't give her the time of day was beyond me. Just seeing how she always walked around with a smile on her face was enough to make anyone's day brighter.

Sou's warm brown eyes twinkled. "You two go wash up for dinner. It'll be out in a moment," she said.

Arizu and I nodded in unison and left to wash our hands. Arizu skipped down the corridors on the way to the bathroom next to the dining room. We took turns washing and then finally made it to our destination. We had just taken our seats when my parents walked in.

My father was a tall man, broad shouldered, and muscular. He sported a beard that was the same reddish-brown as his hair, and the ears of his Dingo heritage flicked proudly atop his head.

My mother was quite a different site to behold. A serious looking woman, she was small and lithe, with long dark hair that fell below her waist and dark, unblinking eyes that matched my own.

When two separate hybrid Lyvens married and had a child, such as my parents, the child would only take on the animal of one of the parents. I had, obviously, taken on the snake side of my family and would inherit the Coluber Legacy.

My parents only acknowledged Arizu's presence after having sat down and made themselves comfortable.

"We weren't expecting you," my father said flatly.

I saw Arizu shrink beneath his gaze. I wanted to speak up in her defense. I wanted to tell my parents to back off and leave her alone. I wanted to, but I didn't. Couldn't. Even though I had the courage to stand up to Avo and her fellow bullies, my parents were a different matter.

I looked down in shame as Arizu struggled to give her explanation under the scrutinizing gazes of my mother and father. "Oh, uh, heh. Well, I thought it'd be okay-"

My mother cut Arizu off. "You thought wrong. Never come to our house without first sending word again."

My cousin nodded meekly and hunched down in her seat. I felt awful seeing her ears droop.

"Now, Roxlin." I looked at my father as he began to speak to me. "Why didn't you let us know as soon as she came here?" I noticed that he didn't even bother to use Arizu's name.

"I didn't see it necessary, Father," I replied. He stared me down, and though I didn't look away, I felt myself sink into my chair a little further.

"Well, next time you decide what's necessary or unnecessary on an important matter such as this without consulting us, there will be consequences," my mother said.

"Yes, Mother." Thankfully the food arrived just then, and we all finished the meal in silence.

Chapter 3
Arizu

"Well, that was nerve-wracking." I flopped onto Roxlin's bed, kicking off my shoes as I went down. "I'm sorry I got you into trouble."

Roxlin shrugged and sat next to me on the bed. She leaned back on her hands and looked at the ceiling. "No need to apologize. There was no reason for them to get so worked up."

"Nah. They had every reason to be angry. I *did* just come without any warning. By the way, why *didn't* you immediately tell your parents I had come?"

"Maybe because an over-active Canine Lyven dragged me to the park as soon as she popped up?" I gave a small chuckle.

Usually after sending word to my grandparents, they would pass along my coming to my aunt and uncle via the Gate. But it had been a spur-of-the-moment visit, and my father and I had only let Paryle and Jaspes know after we had already left to get to their house.

"Yeah, I guess that's true. Still though. It hadn't crossed my mind, but it must have crossed your mind that they'd be angry if you didn't tell them."

"You're right. It did cross my mind. But honestly, I didn't think they'd get so mad. It's not like you're a stranger, nor had they specifically told you to let us know before coming. The real question is, why did you come without any word? School is out right now for fall here in Cillium, but you should still be in school on Earth."

I sat up beside Roxlin and clasped my hands. "It was really just a sudden decision. My dad. . . He told me that he wanted me to stop coming to Cillium."

"He said what now?" Roxlin asked incredulously.

"Yeah, I couldn't believe it. He knows how much coming here means to me. Not only are you here, it's where my mom was from. I didn't understand, and we got into a fight. At the end of the argument, I told him that I wanted to come here. To my surprise, he allowed me to. Maybe he thought that we both just needed some time to cool off and think about the whole situation. I don't know. It was just. . . Not ever coming back here was such a hard thought."

"Well," Roxlin began bluntly, "you do realize that you'll have to pick where you're gonna live permanently someday, right? Paryle and Jaspes won't be around to manage the Gate forever." I did realize this. And I chose to ignore it. At least, for the time being.

We sat in silence for a moment. I was never good at being serious for long periods of time, though. I jumped up from the bed and spun around to face Roxlin. I pointed a finger at her. "I remember that you beat me at Poker last time I was here. Let's grab Sou and play a couple hands! I bet that you won't win this time!"

Roxlin raised an eyebrow. "Avoiding the subject, are we?

Fine. I'll let it slide for now since we've had a long day. But you're gonna have to answer it at some point."

I looked Roxlin straight in the eyes. "I know."

She returned my stare, then stuck out her arm. "Well, then help me up and let's go get Sou. You'd better be prepared to lose and have to clean my room for a week again."

I laughed. "We'll see!"

———●———

That night, after a crushing defeat by both Sou and Roxlin, I laid awake in my bed, tossing and turning. Roxlin was right. I would have to choose where to live permanently soon. Although I knew this, I just really didn't want to have to face it. Unable to sleep, I sighed and finally climbed out of bed. My feet sank into the plush, blue carpet of my room as I headed towards my large window.

My bedroom was the identical shape and size of my cousin's. It was spacious, with the large four-poster bed pushed against the wall to the right of the bedroom door. A bathroom was to the left, and a large closet sat to the right of that, both across the room from my bed. Unlike Roxlin's room though, I hadn't hung any posters or pictures. Hardly anything signified that someone lived in the room. The only way to tell it was my room was because the walls and ceiling were painted my favorite color, sky blue.

Once I reached my window, I opened it quietly and silently climbed outside. My room was right next to Roxlin's, and after having gotten her into trouble earlier that night, I really didn't want to wake her up and disturb her.

Stepping onto luscious green grass, I breathed in the cold, crisp air. I didn't like being cold, though, so I always wore warm pajamas and only barely noticed the cold.

Our rooms were situated on the first story of her parents' mansion, so Roxlin and I both had a direct view into the beautiful backyard garden.

Rose bushes lined the tall white picket fence that stood sentry around the spacious backyard. Stone arches marked the cobblestone paths between fluffy hedges, and the trickling of a fountain could be heard farther back in the garden.

I tiptoed along the stone paths, my feet hardly making a sound. I could see the white puffs of my breath, and felt instantly at peace. The colors of the many different plants under the violet sky seemed so vibrant. It was hard to stay worried in such a peaceful place. Suddenly, a disturbing smell reached my sensitive nose. It was the stench of decay.

I followed the smell, a sinking feeling in my gut. In all my years visiting this garden, I had never smelt decay. I curved along the paths, twisting right and left, before ending up in the center of the garden where the fountain was. I watched the water for a moment. It looked perfectly crystal clear and free of any foul material. I continued along the scent trail until I was directly behind the fountain. To my horror, I found the source of the smell of decay.

Black and completely dead grass spread out from where I stood, barefoot, on the stone path. A substance that looked like melted rubber oozed and bubbled on the ground. I stared at the scene, shocked. What was this? What was happening to the garden?

"Well, would you look at that. The Corruption has spread this far now." A voice suddenly rang out to the right of me.

I spun quickly towards the voice and took a fighting position. The Lyven who greeted me was short and spindly, almost as if malnourished. She crouched down beside me, looking at the oozing mass of blackness and dead grass.

After realizing that she wasn't going to attack me, I straightened back up. "Who are you?" I asked suspiciously.

Moonlight glinted on her vibrant red hair and a pair of fox ears as the woman looked up at me. She stared at me for a moment with her large, green eyes before returning to her inspection of the decayed grass. The woman pulled a small vial out of her pocket and emptied its liquid onto what she had called the "Corruption".

Finally, she spoke again. "A friend." She stood up. Although looking to be a good ten years older than me, she barely came up to my chin at her full height. "My name is Kiara. That's all you need to know for now." The woman turned away and was swallowed up in the shadows of the tall hedges.

"Wait!" I called out. "What do you mean by "right now"? What is this stuff killing the grass? You were here inspecting it, weren't you? Why? And what did you pour onto the grass?"

But the Fox Lyven was already gone.

I took one more look at the worrisome grass before heading back to my room. For a time, I debated on whether or not I should wake someone and show them the appalling sight, but finally decided it would be best to wait until morning. It wasn't like the disturbing scene was going anywhere.

———◦◦◦◦◦———

"It's right on the other side of the fountain." I led Roxlin and her mom, Viern, toward the spot of oozing, melted, rubber-like mass and decayed grass that I had seen the night before. But when we rounded the fountain, I gasped at what was before me. The grass was completely normal – green and thriving. No weird substance was bubbling among dead stalks, and the air smelled completely normal as well.

"I should have known this was just the qualms of a half-Lyven with an over-active imagination. What a waste of time." Viern gave me a scalding glare before stomping away, leaving Roxlin and me alone in the garden.

Although used to the discrimination, I still flinched at her jab calling me a "half-Lyven." Thankfully, it didn't seem as if Roxlin had seen my reaction. I quickly began talking. "You believe me though, right, Roxlin?"

"Yeah," she replied. "We've known each other for most of our lives, and you'd never just make something like this up. Especially if you were sure enough about it to get Mother in-volved. But the question is, why isn't the grass as you said it was?"

The liquid that the Lyven named Kiara had dumped onto the grass crossed my mind. "Well, I think I might know. You see, there was actually a Fox Lyven here last night as well."

Surprise crossed Roxlin's face. "Why didn't you tell this information to my mother?"

I shrugged. "It just, *didn't feel right to*. Weird, right? But, I feel like it's necessary. Could you please keep it a secret from your mom?" After my cousin nodded her assent, I continued. "Anyways, this Fox Lyven said that her name was Kiara and that she was a friend. She poured some sort of liquid onto the grass and then left. Maybe that's what made it all go back to normal? I asked her more questions, but she didn't say anything else."

Roxlin's face was contemplative. "I don't know any Fox Lyvens by the name of Kiara. She's either Lower-Class or not from Avera. Hmm. What did she look like?"

I described her to Roxlin. The Fox Lyven's description wasn't familiar to my cousin, though, and no light was cast upon the mysterious woman.

"Well," my cousin started as we walked back to the house, "at least I know what she looks like so that I can keep an eye out for her. Are you still sure that you don't want to tell my parents that a strange Lyven was in the garden with you last night? They have a lot more resources at their disposal to find her."

I nodded. "Even if I spoke up now, they'd probably just accuse me of being in cahoots with the Fox because I hadn't said anything before. And I still feel like her presence should be kept a secret. Plus, I'm not really trying to find her. Sure, I'm curious about what that "Corruption" was and how she's involved with it. But she seems to have made it go away, so I don't think she means any harm to anyone."

"Well. . . Alright then. I trust your judgment this time."

I smiled. "Thanks, Roxlin!"

"Hmph. Just know that me keeping your secret adds another week of you cleaning my room to the week you already owe me from losing Poker last night."

"Ah man. Seriously?" I complained with a laugh. "You're gonna kill me! When I clean, you specifically don't clean up after yourself which makes extra work for me!"

"Exactly." Roxlin gave wicked grin that only a Snake Lyven could pull off.

The rest of the day was uneventful. Roxlin and I mostly played video games in her room and slacked off any responsibility as was the usual when I visited.

I didn't know how long I would stay this visit. Most of the time it was only a month, but a month didn't seem like it would be long enough this time. I didn't really enjoy living on either Earth or Cillium due to being an outcast. The only reasons I had to be in either world were my family; my grandparents and father on Earth, and Roxlin and Sou on Cillium. I knew my dad wanted me to stay on Earth with him, but Grandma Paryle and Grandpa Jaspes had always stated that I should be among the Lyvens. It was one of the reasons my grandparents and dad didn't get along. When the time came to choose, where would I stand? This question plagued me for the next few days as Roxlin and I just hung around her parents' mansion.

On the fifth day of my visit, I awoke very early in the morning from a nightmare and couldn't get back to sleep. I decided to get something to drink and slipped out of bed. I tiptoed pass Roxlin's bedroom and continued to stealthily stalk the halls to the kitchen, not wanting to take any chances of accidentally waking someone up.

Just as I was passing through the main living room on my way to the kitchen, my sensitive ears picked out a conversation that seemed to concern me.

"- and yes I understand. But it's getting really hard to keep putting up with the half-bred mutt." The voice belonged to my aunt, Viern. Her voice was faint, seeing as it was coming from a closed room from across where I was standing. But I heard well enough. She was practically shouting. "The only reason we allow her to stay here is because of her grandparents. Most Lyvens think it's because she's our niece, but I know that you couldn't care less for her either. You said so yourself that you see her as the reason your sister is dead! And to me she's just a pain in the tail. Honestly, Cillium would be better off without-"

I didn't let myself hear the rest of that sentence. I ran as quickly and as quietly as I could back to my room, getting a drink of water forgotten. The tears pouring down my cheeks was enough water for me right then.

I had already known that my aunt and uncle thought poorly of me. I had known this from the beginning.

So why did it still hurt so much to hear that I was so despised?

Chapter 4
Roxlin

A week had passed since Arizu had come to Cillium. And for the past two days, I had been even more worried about my cousin than usual. Something seemed to have happened that had affected her in a way I had never seen before. She was quieter, more subdued. Even when it was just the two of us. Yet the most concerning thing was that she had barely eaten any of her food during our meals. We were together practically every moment of the day, so I had no idea what could have happened. I would have blamed the incident with the Fox Lyven if Arizu hadn't actually started acting weird a whole two days later.

We were laying on the grass of our secret hideout in the garden on the eighth day of her visit when I had finally had enough of her strange behavior. I sat up to confront her. "Alright. Enough of this. What's wrong?"

Arizu tilted her head to the side. "What do you mean?" She blinked questioningly up at me with wide, brown eyes.

"I mean, why have you been acting so weird lately? You aren't bouncing around like usual, and you're freaking me out with how little you've been eating the past few days."

Arizu gave a bright smile and said, "Have I? I'm sorry, then! But trust me, there's no reason to fret. Everything is good!"

Shock shot through me. Arizu always looked someone in the eyes when she spoke unless she was distracted by something else. But when she had said "Everything is good", she had looked away. She had... *lied*... to me.

For a moment, I couldn't speak. Arizu had never lied to me before. Then I was angry. I grabbed her left fuzzy ear and pulled her up into a sitting position.

"Ow ow ow!" my cousin cried. I let her go and she rubbed her ear crossly. "What in this world did you do that for?"

"*That* was for lying to me. Just last week I said that I trusted you. And now you lie to me all of the sudden?"

Guilt flashed across Arizu's face and she looked away. "Sorry... Don't worry, I'll start acting normal again. No need to get angry."

"No need to get angry?!? Are you serious?! You can't just say that after all of this!"

Arizu turned back and gave a small, sad smile. "Honestly, Rox, it's nothing I'm not used to. I'm just over-reacting to something silly. Really, I don't know why I've been so weird lately!" She hopped up. "Wanna play hide-and-go-seek?"

I sighed. "There you go again dodging any situation that's serious."

Arizu laughed, though it seemed forced. "Well, you know me! I've never been serious for a day in my life!"

I sighed again, knowing that I wouldn't get anywhere with Arizu now. Whatever had happened would have to stay a mystery. For now. Just then, an idea struck me. "How about instead of playing hide-and-go-seek, we instead go get some ice cream?"

Arizu's eyes sparkled at that prospect. "Oh my gosh YES! Let's go!"

We made it through and out of the house uninterrupted. And, when we reached the park, only a few Lyvens whom we didn't know were hanging around. Thankfully, no Avo and gang.

By the time we reached Ulon's Ice Cream, Arizu seemed normal again. But that just made me wonder how much of her happy-go-lucky attitude was a front. And how long that front had been up through the years without me realizing. I pushed those thoughts aside, deciding to leave sleeping beasts lie for the moment.

We entered the ice cream shop and got in line. Ulon's Ice Cream was always efficient and fast no matter how many Lyvens were crowding the small building, and we soon had our regular order of ice cream. As we looked around for an empty table, a slightly familiar voice called out to us.

"Fancy running into you here!" Arizu and I turned to see the kid named (if I remembered correctly), Kaylon. He waved to us from a table next to where we were standing. A girl with long brown hair and horse ears sat across from him. She smiled at us. I wanted to quickly walk away, but it was too late.

"Oh hi!" Arizu said, waving and smiling back. "How have you been? And who's this?" She looked at the Horse Lyven.

"Everything's been going well," Kaylon replied. "And this is my sister, Mina." Mina raised her ice cream cone up in a hello.

"Nice to meet you! I'm Arizu and this is my cousin, Roxlin!" Arizu held out her hand, excited. Thankfully, her excitement seemed genuine. Maybe meeting a new Lyven who may treat her like an actual living creature would help her get out of her stupor.

Mina took her hand and shook it. "Nice to meet you both as well."

"Did you find somewhere to sit? Or would you like to sit with us?" Kaylon asked, gesturing at the two empty seats next to him and his sister.

"We'll find a place to sit. And if we can't, we'll eat outs-. . ."

Arizu cut me off by elbowing me. "Would it really be alright to sit with you guys?"

"Sure," Mina said. My cousin dropped happily into the seat next to her. She took a bite of her ice cream as I grudgingly sat next to Kaylon. Arizu easily struck up a conversation with Mina, and I was stuck eating my ice cream in awkward silence with Kaylon.

"Have you ever tried this birthday cake flavored ice cream?" Kaylon held out his cone for me to see.

I didn't look at it and stared at my cookies n' cream. "Nope."

"Oh my gosh. You haven't?"

"That's what I said, isn't it?" I felt a kick from under the table and looked up at Arizu. She was still talking to Mina. No one would have guessed she'd just kicked me.

I glared at her for a moment, then turned to Kaylon. "No, I haven't. I presume it's good?"

Kaylon smiled and said, "It really is. Wanna try it?"

I looked distastefully at the unfortunately flavored ice cream but tried to keep my voice pleasant as I replied, "No thanks." Another awkward silence ensued. I really wanted to leave, but Arizu looked so happy being able to talk to someone our age without any insults hurled at her. Then it hit me. Mina and Kaylon both looked the same age as Arizu and me. But Kaylon had said they were brother and sister... I glanced at Kaylon. "Hey, you and Mina look the same age?"

Confusion crossed Kaylon's face before he quickly figured out what I meant. He chuckled. "Oh yeah, I didn't mention it before. Mina and I are twins."

That actually surprised me. I had never met twins before, but I had heard that it was impossible for twins to be two separate types of Lyvens. "Isn't that impossible?" I wondered. "She's a Horse Lyven."

"Highly improbable? Yes. Impossible? No. And yes, we know for sure that she's my sister. Even just her eyes are testament of our same genealogy. No full-blown Horse Lyven has eyes like hers."

I hadn't paid attention before, but I looked at Mina's eyes now. I saw, true to Kaylon's words, that her eyes were almost the same color as his. The only difference was that instead of greenish-yellow eyes, she had greenish-brown eyes. Also, they both had slit pupils. "That's really cool. So what are you exactly, then? Alligator or Crocodile?"

"Alligator."

"Cool."

"Yeah." The silence that fell once again was more comfortable now, and him and I finished our ice cream in companionable quiet.

Mina and Arizu were still talking and hadn't finished eating yet, so I brought up one last topic. "You and your sister aren't going to treat Arizu like an outsider?" I asked bluntly.

Kaylon blinked and tipped his head to the side. "Why would we?"

"You heard what the kid said last week about her father being a human. Everyone hates her because of that."

"Really? That's awful. We wouldn't ever do that. Especially over something like that, though that is very strange. She had no control over who her parents are. But, that does explain why. . ." Kaylon didn't finish his thought and instead stared at Arizu intensely.

"What? That explains what?" I asked.

He gave me a sidelong glance. "Well, know that Mina and I are her friends, as well as yours. And, well, I don't like telling anyone what my ability is. . . But I think you need to hear this. . ." Kaylon broke off once again, his eyebrows drawn together.

"Hear what?" I was starting to become frustrated with the way he kept stopping.

Without answering, he stood up and gestured for me to follow him outside.

I stood up to follow. "Hey, Ari," I said before leaving, interrupting my cousin's conversation. She looked up at me questioningly. "Kaylon is gonna show me something real quick. I'll be right back, okay?"

Arizu looked intrigued but only said, "Okay!"

Once outside and standing next to Kaylon, I gave him a hard stare. I didn't fully trust him and was wary of what he was up to. If he tried to attack me, I would smash his head into the ground. "What's going on?" I demanded.

The Alligator Lyven looked around. When he was satisfied that we were alone, he said, "My ability is that I can see one of a Lyven's deepest desires, whether they know of it consciously or not."

I hissed in shock. I didn't like that. I didn't like his ability one bit.

Kaylon held up his hands in a peaceful gesture. "I know, I know. That's why I don't like telling anyone about what my ability is. It sets Lyvens on edge. Anyways, why I'm telling you this is because. . . Well. . . One of Arizu's deepest desires is to be free from emotional pain. And. . . Lyvens, whether half-Lyvens or not, do extreme stuff when they want to be free of pain. I just wanted to tell you this so that you can keep a close eye on her."

A large exhale of breath escaped me, and I leaned against the side of Ulon's Ice Cream. I had known that Arizu was emotionally damaged, so knowing that she wanted to be free from emotional pain wasn't really a surprise. But the implications that this information brought were definitely hard to swallow. I stared at the ground, thinking for a moment. Finally I said, "Thank you for telling me. I won't tell anyone else about your ability. Yours is actually a lot like mine."

"Really? How so?"

I leaned toward him and bared my fangs. "The only thing you need to know is if you're lying to me, I will cover you with spiders."

Kaylon froze at the mention of spiders. "I'll. . . keep that in mind," he said carefully.

When we went back in, Mina and Arizu had finally finished their ice cream, though they were still talking. It seemed my cousin finally had a friend besides me. I was honestly relieved.

"Ready to go?" I asked her.

She gave me a sad look but nodded.

"We should meet up again sometime," Kaylon suggested.

Arizu brightened. "You mean it?" My cousin looked at me excitedly.

"Yeah. Let's do it," I said. Arizu hopped up happily.

Mina followed suit and smiled. "When would that be?" she asked.

"How does Monday next week sound?" Kaylon wondered. "Wanna meet up here?" Everyone else sounded agreement and once outside, our two groups parted ways with quick good-byes.

Arizu and I had just walked up the steps to my parents' house when the door opened and two serious-looking men stepped out. My mother stood in the doorway as the three of them said their farewells. The two men passed Arizu and me without a word and went on their way. But I wasn't paying attention to them anymore. I was looking at my mother. Her face was thunderous as she spotted us. Fear built up in my chest. I quickly smashed that fear down, but nervousness still remained. My mother stepped aside and let Arizu and me in. My cousin didn't seem to notice anything amiss, but I sure did.

"Do you know who those Lyvens were?" My mother asked me as she shut the door. It *clicked* closed with what seemed like the finality of a prison lock.

"No. Are they important?"

My mother's face turned incredulous. "Of course they were important! They were here to see if our family was worthy enough to be invited to a royal ball at the King and Queen's palace!" The entire world of Cillium was actually fairly small – smaller than Earth, even. It was ruled by the benevolent King Rolm and Queen Aulia whom we all were happy to swear fealty to. Arizu had told me that Lyvens had been very blessed with monarchs when compared to Earth.

"That sounds awesome!" Arizu exclaimed. I willed her to stay silent. But she didn't get the memo. "Did you pass the worthiness inspection?"

My mother turned to Arizu, her expression dark. "Not today, no. Thanks to you having dragged my daughter off to who knows where."

"She didn't drag me anywhere," I protested. "I'm the one who-"

"Silence," my mother snapped. I averted my eyes and looked at the ground. "The point is, when we needed you, you were out frolicking about with *her*." My mother gestured to Arizu like she was a discarded piece of meat.

A fire lit inside me. Maybe it was because I was still really worried about my cousin right now. But I had had it with my mother treating her so bad. "I am *so* sorry, Mother. I *completely* forgot to read your mind and know that you needed me here today for an interview. Next time, I'll be *sure* use an ability I don't have to find out."

Without warning, my mother backhanded me across the face. Anger turned her features ugly. A growl sounded from where Arizu stood to the right of me and, before I could stop her, my cousin had leaped in front of me. White teeth flashed as Arizu clamped them squarely onto my mother's retreating hand. With a cry of pain, she lashed out with her other hand, catching Arizu across the face as well. She stumbled a few steps back, clutching her now bloody left hand. Arizu stood in front of me, still growling, and not at all fazed after being smacked by my mother.

I grabbed her shoulder in alarm. "Are you insane, Ari? What in this world are you doing?! Back off!" But it was too late.

"Get out," my mother spat at Arizu. "A disgusting half-breed like you is no longer welcome in this house."

Chapter 5
Arizu

After having told me to get out, Aunt Viern stormed away. Probably to get her bleeding hand looked at. I turned around to see if Roxlin was okay only to have her smack me upside the head. Though it didn't particularly hurt, I still flinched back, shocked. I placed a hand where she had struck me, another, though different, pain to my already throbbing face.

"What were you *thinking?*" my cousin asked furiously. "If you had just stayed quiet, everything would have turned out fine. Now I have to figure out a way to fix this." Roxlin started pacing back and forth across the threshold of the front door, arms crossed. I stared at her meekly as she muttered different options under her breath.

"I can try to convince Mother to let her stay, but that's about as likely to happen as me turning into a Falcon Lyven. It wouldn't matter if I refuse to let her kick Ari out because she can just get Father to haul her out. Father would do it. If Ari goes through the Gate to Earth, then Mother would most likely cut off the connection and make it so that Ari could never return here." Suddenly, Roxlin punched the frame on the side of the door, cracking the wood. I cowered, a little scared at the Snake Lyven's display of anger. I had never seen her like this before. She was usually very calm and collected.

After a minute of silence, I asked tentatively, "Roxlin, are you alright?"

She ignored my question and still faced away from me even as she said, "The best option for you right now is to leave and let Mother cool down. While you're gone, I'll somehow convince her to allow you to live here again. You're actually lucky she's just kicking you out and doing nothing more. She has grounds to kill you for you attacking her like that."

I lowered my head, sadness and regret flooding through me. It had been so stupid of me to act so impulsively. But seeing Aunt Viern hit my cousin and best friend, let alone her own child, had made me so mad.

When Roxlin turned around, she was composed once again. "Let's go. We need to get you out of here as soon as possible in case Mother decides to give you an even more severe punishment." Roxlin began leading the way to where our bedrooms were.

"You mean, I really have to leave and be all by myself?" I asked in a small voice.

Roxlin didn't stop and didn't turn around. "You can't hide here, even in the garden. Mother would find you. You have to leave and get away from here for your safety. And...yeah. I can't go with you. Think about it. If you leave by yourself, no one would try to find you. But if I went with you, you can bet your life that Mother and Father would track me down, which would lead them to you. Say they claim you kidnapped me. Not only would no one listen to my side of the story, no one would question if my parents decided to kill you on a claim like that. Like I said, you leaving here by yourself is the best option."

I was taken aback by how Roxlin seemed to have thought out every single situation in the space of a few minutes. I was still trying to wrap my mind around being kicked out of the house.

When we reached my room, Roxlin told me that she would grab a bag for me to throw what I needed in to while I started gathering the things I wanted to take with me.

Everything was going too fast. Nothing was making sense. The world seemed to continue to speed up until I was back at the front door. Then, time seemed to freeze for a moment as I stood with a backpack strapped onto my back and holding an overstuffed duffle bag. I felt tears well up in my eyes. I didn't want to go. If I did have to leave here, I wanted to at least go back through the Gate to Grandma Paryle and Grandpa Jaspes. But according to Roxlin, if I did that, I would probably be blocked from ever returning to Cillium. And that would crush me.

As I stood there crying and sniffling, unable to say anything, Roxlin reached out and patted me on the head. "Don't cry," she said sternly. "Tears don't solve anything. Smiling suits you much better." She handed me a piece of paper, opened the front door, and ushered me outside. "Don't forget to find somewhere to get ice to put on your face so that it doesn't swell up more than it already has, okay?"

I nodded as I wiped away my tears. My throat felt too

choked for me to say anything. So I instead just turned away, preparing myself for my journey into Avera without the only true friend I had ever had.

"And," I heard Roxlin say behind me. "Stay safe."

I turned back around, gave a big smile that I didn't feel, and then headed off. I instinctively headed for Ulon's Ice Cream, deciding on the way that the ice cream shop would probably be the best place to find something cold for my face. On the way, I took a look at the note Roxlin had given me. It read,

Don't forget that Mina, Kaylon, you, and I are meeting up at Ulon's Ice Cream on Monday. I expect you to be there.

I smiled at the note. It was nice to know that even with me having screwed everything up, Roxlin was still looking out for me. I knew deep down that she always would.

The park wasn't too crowded when I got there, and neither was Ulon's Ice Cream. I was able to go straight up to the counter and ask if they had some ice I could put on my face. They did, and I ordered a bowl of chocolate ice cream to eat while I held the ice pack to my puffy cheek.

While I sat at one of the small tables, I had time to think of what I should do. I could stay here in the park somewhere, but it was quite close to my aunt and uncle's mansion. I didn't think it would be smart for me to stay so close, but at the same time, I didn't want to go too far away. Who knew what would happen to me if I wandered too far off? An idea suddenly struck me.

What if I tried finding that Fox Lyven I had met in the garden? I was very curious about what she had said that night. Sure, it was probably not wise to look for her because

I had no idea where she was or how far away she could be, but I had nothing else to do while I waited for Monday to come. And if my search seemed like it would lead me out of the city, I would give up. Also, I did have an inkling of how to find her. The smell of the "Corruption" she had talked about had been very strong and distinct. While looking around the area I could try to pick up that smell. If she was searching for the "Corruption" to make it go away like on the night I met her, this would be my best chance at finding her. I didn't know if the Fox Lyven had even been seeking out the Corruption, let alone trying to fix the problem. But this plan was better than sitting around for three days doing nothing.

Oh yeah, I suddenly remembered. *Kiara was her name, if I'm correct.* I looked at the sky through the ice cream shop's window. Violet hues were swallowing the pink. It was getting late, I realized. I would need to find a place to eat a real dinner and sleep before starting my search in the morning.

Having set a goal in mind, I finished my ice cream quickly. I thanked the clerk for giving me the ice pack and then left to find a fast food place and a hotel.

Since money wasn't what counted in the Lyven's society, I was able to grab some dinner and secure a room in a hotel about a mile from the park with no trouble. I bitterly wondered if the receptionist at the desk would have given me a room if she had known I was half human.

After finishing my food and getting ready for bed, I wished – not for the first time – that I had just been born either a full-blooded human or a full-blooded Lyven. Not only would I most likely not be an outsider on either Earth or Cillium, I wouldn't have to choose between the two worlds.

But I quickly pushed that line of thinking away, just like always. I was born as I was born, and wishing wasn't going to change anything.

Having finished getting ready for sleep and turning out the lights, I climbed into bed. I laid there staring at the darkness, still numb from the day's events. I had been distracted by other things after having left Roxlin's mansion, so it was only now that the true force of my predicament hit me.

If my aunt and uncle never allowed me to live with them and be around Roxlin anymore, there would be no reason for me to stay in Cillium. And if I made the decision to leave, it would most likely be for the last time.

Just like my cousin had said earlier, crying wasn't going to help anything. Even so, I felt tears roll down my face once again as I realized just how lonely and insignificant I felt. This wasn't the first time I had cried myself to sleep. But it was the first time I cried myself to sleep wondering if there was even a point to this hardship called "life."

⸺⸙⸺

Waking up with the sun, I felt better than I had last night. I answered my own question from the night before as I got ready to leave. Of course there was a point to life! Otherwise, why would any Lyven or human be on their planet? I just needed to find the purpose of my own life. And I would! I was sure of that.

I took a deep breath of the chilly morning air once outside. I was excited to start searching! If the Fox Lyven tried to disappear like she had the night we met in the garden, I would follow her. But, of course, that was all dependent on whether I could even find her or not. Maybe the Corruption had only been in my aunt and uncle's garden. It didn't seem like that would be the case, but it could very well be.

I started my search by making a full circle around the hotel, sniffing the whole time. Finding nothing, I continued up the street, catching a ride in what was the equivalent of a taxi on Earth. I wouldn't be able to smell anything from outside, but this was definitely a quicker and less tiring way to get to my destination than walking.

I was headed toward the central dome of Avera that held a giant garden inside. I didn't know where the Corruption lurked, but since I had found it in a garden, I thought that looking in another garden would be a logical place to check.

Lyvens prided themselves on their ability to keep a healthy environment everywhere, unlike humans. Where Roxlin's mansion was located, it was practically what you would call on Earth a "wildlife reservation" even though it was considered normal scenery on Cillium. Even though tall buildings lined and crowded the streets here in central Avera much like in New York City, no smog polluted the air. Lyvens had found a way to make vehicles that resembled cars and planes without using material that destroyed the planet, and any machines that needed it ran on environmentally friendly fuel. To honor those achievements, most large cities had a Garden Dome located in the center of them like the one I was heading to.

The Avera Garden Dome was full of exquisite and rare plants that usually didn't grow in the climate here. Though

Cillium was a small planet, all different climates were spread all around. Which made sense, seeing as Lyvens were animal hybrids of all kind.

On the ride to the Avera Garden Dome, I had time to think once again about how lonely I felt. But I mentally slapped myself and put a smile on my face. Everything was going to work out fine! Roxlin said she'd somehow convince Aunt Viern to let me live with them again, and I trusted Roxlin. In the meantime, I had a hunt to commence.

After thanking my driver, I turned and faced the Avera Garden Dome. It was large, as tall and wide as a five-story building. Built from a glass-like substance, it was see-through. Not that you could really see much from outside. Blue, green, and white vine-like plants grew along the perimeter and up the side, making it so that you couldn't see much of anything else. I headed inside. Although I had been inside before, the sight of the beautiful garden still took my breath away.

Purple flowers the color of the night sky grew along the polished stone path while a little farther back were the Crystal Roses that only grew naturally in the coldest Cillium climates. They were my favorite flowers. Their pristine petals glowed in the sunlight filtering in, and the daylight's pink tinge turned the Crystal Roses a pinkish hue. The crystal made the light that fell through cast an array of beautiful patterns across the ground.

Among the other wonderful plants, placed in the center of the dome, was a giant white tree standing sentry. Black markings ran along its bark, and emerald leaves fluttered in a breeze that blew from special climate controlling machines.

Avera Garden Dome workers were always about, tending the plants and making sure they thrived. But today, all of the workers were gathered around a certain patch of Crystal Roses just past the center tree. Their dark gray uniforms made them easy to spot. That's when a familiar, decaying scent reached my nostrils. I hurried over to the huddled group of workers. I tapped one on the shoulder.

"What's going on?" I asked.

The Lyven started, turning around to face me. Apprehension was plastered on his face. "Oh, um. Well, this isn't for non-Garden Dome employees to know about, so why don't you take a look at the other parts of the garden for a little bit before we close it down for the day. Okay?"

Now that I was so close, the smell wafting from dead and dying plants and that weird bubbling substance almost made me physically sick. Not heeding the worker's words, I pushed through the throng. Sure enough, when reached the front, the exact same sight I had seen about a week ago greeted me.

"Hey, you can't be here right now!" another employee urgently griped. She grabbed my arm and turned me away from the depressing view.

"That's what I told her," the first Lyven I had originally spoken to said, coming to stand next to the lady holding my arm. I tore my arm free from the her grasp.

"There's a Fox Lyven named Kiara that can fix this," I said to the group of employees. I actually didn't know for sure if she had been the one to cure my aunt and uncle's garden of this death and destruction, but I didn't want to be kicked out when I had just found my best bet at seeing that Fox Lyven once again. So I needed a reason to stay here. And this bluff worked well. I was about to say more to convince the workers when a laugh cut me short.

A small, wiry figure pushed through the group until she stood before me. The Fox Lyven known as Kiara looked up at me. She grinned. "Looking for me?"

Chapter 6
Roxlin

After shutting the door on Arizu's retreating back, I stood there staring at nothing in particular. My thoughts raced for a moment until my mother suddenly appeared next to me, materializing from what seemed like thin air. Her ability was being able to practically turn invisible in any shadow large enough to cover her slender frame, whether sunlight shone near or not.

"Huh. I really thought you'd put up more of a fight about getting rid of her," Mother said, her left hand now bandaged.

Because I was used to her ability, her sudden appearance didn't faze me one bit. "Would there have been any point to me putting up a fight?" I snapped. I immediately regretted saying that and flinched back instinctively, preparing for a blow. But my mother just stood there, contemplating something.

"I was actually quite impressed with how you handled this situation. You thought about all plausible possibilities and came up with the best course of action. Well done."

I looked away, disgusted. Was that really all my mother

cared about? She truly, honestly wasn't worried about Arizu wandering around Avera all by herself *at all?*

"Anyways," Mother said, changing the topic. Like her tossing Arizu out wasn't important enough to think about for long. "Those men from the palace will be back tomorrow morning. Now that you don't have such a big distraction, I expect you to be well dressed and on your best behavior for their interview. Earlier, they ran out of time waiting for you to be back from wherever that half-breed had dragged you off to. So don't be late, either. They will be here at ten o'clock sharp." With that, my mother disappeared into shadow once again.

I felt like punching something again, but my hand hurt. And my face hurt. I needed to follow my own advice and get some ice to put on both wounds. I touched the throbbing area of my face tenderly and felt swelling on my left cheekbone.

This wasn't the first time I had been hit by my mother. A word out of line could usually be tolerated, but if open insubordination was shown, it was quickly stifled. Being very strong-willed and stubborn, I had learned this the hard way as a child.

I sighed and headed to the kitchen. Once there, I put ice in a bag and held it to my cheek with my hurt hand, hoping the ice would help both wounds at the same time.

I sat on one of the counters, bored. It was usually always boring in this house without Arizu doing and saying random stuff. I wondered how she was faring right now. Knowing her, she was probably eating ice cream at Ulon's Ice Cream. That appetite of hers was ridiculous.

After some time, kitchen workers came in to prepare dinner. I didn't feel like eating, so I tossed the rest of the ice away and left to my room. I was tired, and worrying about how Arizu was getting along just made me even more tired. I was sure she'd be fine. Yeah, she was immature. But she wasn't a child. And she wasn't stupid, either. She'd be fine.

I pushed away my worry for the moment, focusing instead on getting ready for bed. I had my own troubles to deal with. Namely, that interview in the morning.

According to Mother, only the ones deemed worthy by the Lyvens that who had visited earlier would be invited to a ball thrown by the Queen and King of Cillium. Although it was quite a great honor, the whole thing seemed fishy. Why now? No major holidays were anytime soon. What purpose was this ball serving besides bringing together powerful Lyvens? And if they wanted a bunch powerful Lyvens that weren't already at the palace to come, why not just send a formal request asking for their presence? It didn't make sense. These thoughts plagued me as I climbed into bed and tried to sleep.

Unlike Arizu who could sleep anywhere at any time, I had trouble falling asleep that night. Tossing and turning, I was finally able to drift off into a dreamless slumber.

⸺ ◉ ⸺

I awoke to a hand on my shoulder. I looked up to see Sou staring down at me.

The Bear Lyven smiled. "Good morning, young Master!"

she said. "It's about an hour until the meeting. I came to wake you up so that you wouldn't be late. I'm sure you know how angry your mother was about you missing it yesterday."

I touched my tender cheek and gave a snort of laughter. "Yeah. I know."

Sou gave me a troubled look. "I'm so sorry about what happened, Roxlin. I know how close you and Arizu are. Do you think she'll be alright on her own?"

I sat up and stretched before standing up and grabbing some clothes from my closet. "Even if she isn't going to be fine on her own, it's not like we can do anything about it. The best we can do for right now is to stay on my parents' good side and somehow coerce them into allowing Arizu to live here again."

"You're right," Sou said with a forced smile. "Well, I'll let you get ready." She moved her portly bulk towards the door.

"Thank you for waking me up," I said. "And, would mind making me some pancakes for breakfast?" Arizu had introduced pancakes to me a while ago, and they had quickly become one of my favorite meals.

"Of course not," Sou replied. And with that, she left.

After taking a quick shower, it only took about ten minutes for me to get ready the rest of the way. I checked myself over in the mirror to make sure I met my mother's standards.

Though not my preference, I wore a dress the color of the night sky. I shared my mother's slender form, and the tight bodice showed that off. The skirt fell nicely from the waist to my knees, and sleeves came to just before my elbows. The purple of the dress complemented my long, straight, black hair.

Satisfied with the dress, I brushed through my hair once more and took a simple white hairpin to pin my bangs up, the white a nice contrast to the rest of me. I slipped on a pair of flats that matched the color of my dress. One more look-over, and I headed to the kitchen.

Sou greeted me there with a fresh plate of pancakes. Butter melted atop them and syrup glistened in a bottle on the counter.

"Lady Viern was displeased that you missed breakfast," the Bear Lyven told me while I poured syrup on my pancakes and began to eat.

I looked at her in surprise, chewing a large mouthful. "Really?" I asked around the bite. I usually never ate breakfast with my mother and father, so it was curious as to why she would be bothered with me not showing up this morning. I could see her being bothered by me skipping dinner the night before, but not breakfast. It could be because of what happened last night, but why would that have changed anything? I brushed the comment aside.

"Oh well. What is she gonna do? Kick me out?" I shoved another large bite of food into my mouth.

"Maybe not," Sou said with a worried expression. "But you should still be careful of what you say and do. Especially right now."

I waved my fork at her. "I know, I know. No need to get so worked up." I quickly finished my meal, the time for the meeting almost here. I left the dishes for Sou to clean up and headed to the front living room. I was the first one there.

I sat in one of the plush arm chairs and waited for the rest of my family to arrive. My mother and father came in together, well dressed in a way that was certainly eye-catching, but not too formal.

Mother wore a black pencil skirt that hugged her hips and a white, frilly blouse was tucked into it. Black high heels completed her outfit, and her hair was pulled half up and half down.

Father's dress shirt, perfectly creased pants, and dress shoes were all black. A white tie finished his outfit.

Everything about them screamed crisp articulateness, and I was so glad I chose to wear purple instead of my usual black. I didn't want to match them. The three of us had no time to talk before the doorbell rang. Father hurried to open it.

Two men dressed in suits entered. Both were tall and imposing. One was an Eagle Lyven, and the other a Leopard Lyven. To me, it looked like the Leopard Lyven was second-in-command and also more laid back. The Eagle Lyven, however. . .

His golden-brown eyes scoured over the three of us, staring with apparent disdain. Ruffling his feathery-looking brown hair, he cleared his throat. "As far as introductions go since you weren't here yesterday," he shot me a contemptuous glance. "My name is Selen, and this is my partner, Kren." Selen gestured to the Leopard Lyven. Kren gave me a small smile that flashed white against his dark skin. The smile seemed to say, 'Sorry about my partner. He's a little rude.'

"Where's the last member?" Selen asked my parents, not bothering to hear my own introduction.

Mother and Father exchanged a confused look.

"What do you mean?" my mother asked. "You said you

would interview us today when our family was all together. The only other member of this family is my daughter." My hand clenched into a fist at that remark, but I didn't say anything. Selen sighed, rolling his eyes as he did.

"I heard that you were supposed to be cunning and smart, Lady Viern. Apparently, those were only rumors." Both my parents bristled at that, but both surprisingly held their tongues. I hid a smile. "Where's the girl, Arizu?"

"She's not a member of this household," Mother hissed.

The Eagle Lyven wore an annoyed expression. He spoke slowly, as if to a child. "Last time I checked, your husband's sister had a child with a human. Being such kind rulers, the King and Queen allowed the child to spend time here in Cillium despite her heritage. And since you were her closest relatives in Cillium, she was placed here in this household for you to watch over. So yes, she *is* a part of this "*household*.""

Mother looked at a loss at the moment. Father stepped in. "She's. . . not here right now," he said hesitantly.

Selen rubbed his temples. "Of *course* she isn't. Great. You Lyvens are officially useless. If it were up to me, you would *not* be invited to the royal ball. But unfortunately, I just received word today from the monarchs themselves that your family gets a free pass to attend. Why I wasn't informed of this before coming to Avera, I have no idea. I would have objected profusely."

"That's probably exactly why you *weren't* told," Kren spoke for the first time, his voice a deep rumbling that took me by surprise. He smiled lightheartedly as Selen glared at him.

"Needless to say, Kren and I mostly came by today to

tell you this and to let you know that the ball is set to be in a month's time. You are invited to stay at the palace until the date. You have a week to gather your things and arrive at the palace. We expect *all* family members to be there." With that, Selen promptly left our house while Kren waved good-bye on his way out.

Mother seemed coiled with anger, ready to spring at the merest little thing. I was about to say a witty remark about the meeting we'd just had, but I didn't think it would be appreciated at that moment. I calmly slunk away from my mother as my father tried to cool her down.

I was just about to make my escape when my mother's gaze snapped to me. "Roxlin!" She practically yelled even though I was still fairly close by. "Find that half-breed and get her back here. Now!"

"Yes, Mother." I barely managed to keep the anger from my voice. I quickly returned to my room, kicking off my shoes as I entered.

Mother didn't know about my meeting with Kaylon, Mina, and Arizu on Monday. I planned to keep it that way. I would pretend to look for Arizu, but I would really just wait until I saw her then. I could bring her back home after some ice cream. Monday was the day after tomorrow, and we had a week to get to the palace. It would all work out.

With that, I quickly changed back into my usual black plants and black shirt. I then proceeded to exit my room via my window, entering the garden. My bare feet sank into the springy, green grass and I breathed in the familiar sweet aroma of flowers. I walked through the small labyrinth of hedges to get to the secret spot where Arizu and I usually spent most of our time when outside. I picked up the book I had left there and flipped to the chapter I was on.

The book was entitled *Blood Ties*. It was a strange title. And so far, there were so many things that the title eluded to in the book that it made my head spin. I was excited for how it would end, but I found it hard to focus at the time.

Many questions raced through my mind about the information I had gathered from the visit that morning. Why had my family suddenly been invited to the royal ball without having to be approved of by Selen and Kren? And why, not that I was complaining, was it specifically pointed out that we needed to bring Arizu with us? Yes, it was thanks to the King and Queen's generosity that Arizu was able to live both here and on Earth. But the monarchs had shown no real interest in my cousin besides requiring my parents to send reports in about if Arizu was obeying Cillium law or not. Besides that, it was as if they saw her as just another Lyven.

After many minutes of not being able to focus on the book, I put it down and lay on the grass. I hated worrying about things. There was no point to it unless there was an actual problem I could solve. But these were just questions, not puzzles. There was no way for me to be able to know the answers unless I asked the King and Queen – like that was ever going to happen.

The lack of sleep the night before caught up to me and before I knew it, I fell fast asleep.

Chapter 7
Arizu

I stared in shock at the sudden appearance of Kiara, a deathly silence having fallen over the group. I really hadn't expected it to be so easy to find her. And yet here she was. Standing in front of me with her hands on her hips. Kiara raised an eyebrow at me, waiting for my explanation as to why I had been searching for her. My stomach decided to growl loudly in response.

It was only then that I realized I hadn't eaten breakfast. Wait, why was I getting distracted about that right now? This wasn't the time for hunger! And yet. . . "I'm hungry. Let's talk over breakfast!" I smiled at Kiara.

The Fox Lyven seemed slightly perplexed at my seeming randomness, but I seriously was hungry. . .

"Alright, then. . . I know a good breakfast cafe near here," she said while leading the way out of the group of workers. I followed happily behind, excited that Kiara wasn't running away, seemed willing to talk, and was leading me to breakfast! It seemed that the original Garden Dome worker who had spoken to me as well as the one who had grabbed my arm were relieved about me leaving. As we left, no one spoke to or stopped Kiara and me.

Once reaching the small cafe, we settled at an outside table farthest from the entrance.

"So," Kiara said once our order came. "Why have you been looking for me?" I took a bite of my food and chewed while gathering my thoughts. Once I swallowed, I said,

"I have a lot of questions I wanted to ask you about that night you were in my aunt and uncle's garden."

"Makes sense," Kiara replied with a dainty bite of her breakfast croissant. "Go ahead and ask." I set my fork down, thrilled.

"Alright! So, what was that stuff you called the "Corruption"?"

"Can't tell you," came the reply. I deflated, confused.

"But you told me I could ask you my questions. . .?"

"Yeah, but I didn't say I'd answer them." Kiara took another dainty bite of her croissant.

"That's not fair though!"

"Life's not fair, kid." She gave me a look as I slumped down in my chair. She then sighed. "Look, kid. You weren't supposed to see what happened that night. I'm sorry that you have a lot of questions, but I can't tell you about stuff you aren't supposed to know yet." I started.

"Yet?" I wondered.

"Yeah, "yet". Like I said back in the garden, all you need to know for right now is that my name is Kiara and that I'm your friend. You'll learn all about the Corruption, among other things, later." Kiara hesitated, then said,

"Well, I guess I can tell you two pieces of information. The first is, you'll learn all about everything when you go to the palace for the royal ball that's taking place in a month's time. The second is that Kaylon and Mina work for me and my partner. They'll protect you while my partner and I are off settling the Corruption down." I was stunned as Kiara threw her croissant onto her plate and got up to leave. I snapped out of my stupor and grabbed her arm as she was about to walk away.

"Wait!" I said desperately, confused. "I'm going to a ball? Kaylon and Mina aren't really friends with me? They're just being nice because you told them to?" Kiara peeled my fingers away from around her wrist.

"Yes, you're going to a ball. Roxlin will tell you about it when you meet her on Monday. And, though I'm not sure why it's important that they're your friends or not, no. From what I've heard from both Kaylon and Mina, they aren't faking being your friends. Yes, they were told to act as guards for you, but they're genuine Lyvens." I fell back in my chair, slightly relieved at the Fox Lyven's words. "Now, if you'll excuse me, I have some Corruption to take care of."

"Thank you for talking to me, Kiara," I said, though still completely confused. With no response, the wiry Fox Lyven disappeared into the crowded walkways of Avera, heading back towards the Garden Dome.

Turning my attention from Kiara, I quickly ate the rest of my breakfast and headed off. I didn't know exactly where I was going, but questions whirling around inside my brain left me not caring.

I had no idea what to do for the next two days. Finding food and places to sleep were no problem, but finding something to *do*, on the other hand.

It ended up that I spent most of my time in an arcade for

the remaining days until Monday. I topped four high scores while I was there. Maybe more. I honestly couldn't remember for sure. But it was definitely at least four...

I arrived at Ulon's Ice Cream right when they were opening, ten o'clock on Monday. It hit me while I was waiting that the four of us hadn't specified a time of meeting. Well, one way or another, I could wait there all day, so it wasn't like I'd miss them. And thus my time of boredom began.

The minutes ticked by so slowly. By the time an hour passed, I had just about died of boredom, so I started a conversation with the clerk.

He was a different Lyven than the one who had given me the ice to put on my cheek three days before. It turned out that he and his wife were Crane Lyvens, and they were expecting their first child any day now. Whenever a costumer came in we'd, of course, have to stop talking. But we talked until *finally*, at two o'clock sharp, a familiar figure strode into the ice cream shop.

"Roxlin!" I shouted happily. I ran over smiling and gave her a hug.

"Ugh. You're so noisy. Let me go," Roxlin said. But even as she peeled me away from her, I could tell that she was happy to see me. "How'd it go being all by yourself in Avera for the first time?" she asked me.

"It was soooooooooo boriiiiiiiiiiinnnnnnng," I told her. "Except-" I hesitated. Should I tell Roxlin that I had tried and found Kiara? Not seeing any reason to not tell her besides getting a scolding, I continued. "Well, I went and searched for that Fox Lyven I met in the garden two weeks ago. I found her, too."

"What?!" Roxlin looked incredulous. "Why would you do that?!"

I shrugged. "I couldn't think of anything else to do. . ." Roxlin was still staring at me as if I were insane as I progressed my story. "Well, I still had questions I wanted answered, too. . . Anyways. I found her at the Avera Garden Dome and we talked for a little bit over breakfast. Get this, Roxlin. She said that she ordered Kaylon and Mina to be my bodyguards."

My cousin at first looked shocked, but her expression soon turned angry. "Why in this world would she do that? That's totally creepy. But I guess it explains why they showed up from out of nowhere and suddenly became our buddies. I knew something was off with them."

Just then, the bell attached to the front door of Ulon's Ice Cream sounded. Kaylon and Mina walked in.

"Speak of the devils," Roxlin mumbled under her breath.

I didn't know what to do. It was worrying as to why I all the sudden had bodyguards, but, even though I knew it wasn't really important right now with so many other strange things going on, I was more concerned with if Mina and Kaylon were really Roxlin's and I's friends. Sure, Kiara had made it sound as if they were. But could I really trust the Fox Lyven?

"So. You've been following Arizu around Avera for the past few days?" Roxlin asked the twins, hostility coating her voice. Neither looked surprised about Roxlin knowing what their job was. But I was surprised that it hadn't even crossed my mind that the two of them might have been following me. If they had been, I'd had no idea!

"Yeah. We took turns keeping an eye on her for you," Kaylon said.

"No, you kept an eye on her because that's what you were told to do. Don't pretend like you care about us," Roxlin shot back.

"Woah, woah," Mina cut in. "It may be our job, but we've been watching you two for a while now, and we both like you guys. We think you're great Lyvens with strong hearts."

"You just made this whole thing seem even creepier than it already was." Roxlin's jaw clenched as she got angrier. "If you have the guts to say stuff like that and think that we'll be okay with it, you're dead wrong. How long has this even been going on?" I placed a calming hand onto Roxlin's shoulder, trying to get her to stop baring her fangs. It looked like she was about to bite Mina's head off.

"Rox, calm down," I said. "Yes, this is very creepy. But if what Mina just said is true and they've been watching us for a while, then maybe they have been protecting us? And if that's true, shouldn't we try to be a little more understanding? Maybe they can explain some stuff to us." Roxlin backed off a little, but I could still feel her tense under my hand.

"We can't trust them," she warned me.

"I'm not saying that we should trust them. But my gut says that we should at least listen to what they say," I replied firmly. "Let's hear what they have to say for themselves." I turned to the twins. "Well?" Kaylon began talking.

"We've only been assigned to look out for Arizu since the last time she came to Cillium. Kiara thought that it would be a good idea to become friends with both of you to make our job easier this time around. It's really hard to watch all the exits of your house with just two people. Although, it does help that you both usually stay at your home or only go to Ulon's Ice Cream."

"But why?" I asked. "Why do I need bodyguards? Why give the job to two teenagers? Who is Kiara, really? What is going on?" Mina spoke now.

"We can't tell you. And about my brother and I being the ones to guard you despite our young age? Let's just say that our Lyven abilities work well together." Roxlin glared, saying,

"And *why* can't you tell us about anything that's going on?" Kaylon looked at my cousin, sympathy showing across his scaled face.

"The group Mina and I belong to is tiny, and the secret it holds is more closely guarded than the King and Queen themselves. My sister and I don't actually know the reason as to why all this is taking place. Heck, I don't even think Kiara or Feyor know the full reason."

"Well, that's just great. You're blindly following some psychos' orders. How do you know that neither of those aforementioned aren't just having you keep an eye on Arizu to, say, know when the best time to murder her is or something?" Kaylon chuckled.

"Feyor is our dad, and Kiara is a close friend of our family's. My sister and I have known both, well, obviously, our whole lives. We trust them, of course. They aren't murderers."

"And you know that how? You don't even know the purpose of the group you're in!" Kaylon hesitated at that.

"There's honestly nothing I can say to you to convince you that we're good Lyvens," Kaylon said. "It was unfair of us to expect you to understand without any facts to back up what we're doing. But I will say, Mina and I will still guard Arizu, as we've been told to do. I hope you both can come to terms with that." Through this conversation, I had stayed silent. I now spoke up.

"I say we give them a chance, Rox. They must have a good reason, right?"

"Ari, you're too trusting," Roxlin snapped. "Why would you ever want to give them a chance after hearing all this?"

"Because I truly feel that it's the right thing to do. I'm still not saying that we should trust them. Just that we should let them try to prove themselves. Plus, isn't it better to keep them where we can see them for most of the time?" I smiled at my cousin. She glared at the twins for a moment longer before sighing and looking away.

"Fine. But if either of you show any signs of harming my cousin or I, I will tear your spines out and shove them down your throats." I gave a snort of laughter as Mina's face paled. One of the twins' fears (most likely Mina's, from her reaction) must be gore or something. Roxlin usually didn't say stuff like that unless she was preying on a Lyven's fear.

Suddenly, Roxlin stiffened.

"What's wro-" I began to ask. But I didn't get to finish my question before the front window to the right of the door of Ulon's Ice Cream burst apart. Glass shards flew across the room. I felt the sting of many cuts across my face and arms and heard cries of pain from the few other costumers in the shop. A dark, lumbering form stood in the now mostly empty window frame as the familiar smell of Corruption smacked into me.

Before I had fully registered what had happened, my

cousin had already tipped a table onto its side and had pulled me behind it next to her.

"Are you okay?" I worriedly tried to look Roxlin over.

"I'm fine. But that's not important right now. What's important is knowing what in the world that *thing* is, and why it just attacked Ulon's shop." Roxlin's voice was strained. It was then I noticed her bleeding from a deep cut on her right shoulder.

"You aren't okay!" I panicked at the sight of all the blood flowing from the wound. "And where is Kaylon and Mina? Are they all right?" I didn't have time to check where the twins had gone, as in one giant leap, the thing that smelled of Corruption flew over the table and landed in front of Roxlin and me. It stood there for a moment, and I was able to get a good look at the horrifying figure.

It was at least seven feet tall and resembled a humanoid, having two arms, two legs, and a head. But that was where the similarities ended. It was covered in the oozing black goo that had been present at both my aunt and uncle's garden and at the Avera Garden Dome. It rippled along the form, bubbling up and popping with a sickening sound. No eyes could be seen through the goop.

It struck then, lightning fast. I only had a split second to realize that its arm was coming straight at me.

Chapter 8
Roxlin

I moved to stop the thing in front of Arizu and I from striking my cousin, but something was faster than me. It was an alligator.

It flew in front of Arizu and clamped its jaws onto the thing's arm. I stared in confusion for a moment before realizing that the alligator must be Kaylon. I used his distraction to grab Arizu's arm and pull her from behind the table to get her away from the monster.

We stumbled away, slipping on broken glass. I tripped over a fallen chair and Arizu and I tumbled to the floor. Landing on my injured right shoulder, I tried to bite my lip to keep from crying out. Unfortunately, all that accomplished was to make my lip bleed.

The monster heard my cry and ran towards my cousin and I, Kaylon still hanging from its arm. But before it could reach us, a large brown horse kicked it right in the midriff. Kaylon let go and landed on his four feet as the thing flew across the room. Thankfully, all other Lyvens in the ice cream shop had escaped by now and were no where to be seen.

"Get on my back!" Mina called to us.

We picked ourselves up and began our stumbling across the chaotic room once again to get to Mina. My head was hazy from the pain caused by my cut shoulder, but I managed to reach the Horse Lyven without any more missteps, Arizu in tow.

Mina knelt down to make it easier for us to climb on just as a thunderous cry sounded from behind the three of us. The disgusting thing had recovered and was charging straight in our direction. Kaylon didn't allow the monster to get very far.

He rushed in front of the monster and grabbed its leg in his jaws. Rolling across the floor, he made the thing fall to the ground. Its leg tore away from its body with a sickening *slurp* as Arizu and I finally got situated onto Mina's back.

Once she stood up, she yelled, "Hold on tight!"

My cousin and I braced ourselves as the Horse Lyven took off. We made it to the broken window in two strides and, without hesitation, Mina sprang through the shattered opening. With that, we were galloping away across the grassy park.

"What about Kaylon?" I called to the racing Lyven.

"He'll be fine," Mina panted between heavy breaths. "The Corrupted will only be trying to get at Arizu, and Kiara will be there to help him take care of it in no time." We spoke no more as Mina continued to race on. We were traveling away from the city, towards the forest that surrounded Avera. Finally, after galloping for around ten minutes, we reached the first line of trees and stopped.

It was a good thing we had, because I almost passed out

from blood loss. Arizu caught me before I slipped to the ground.

"Roxlin!" She cried, panic filling her voice.

I felt her dismount and carefully pull me off of Mina's back. She laid me gently on the ground as the edges of my vision began to fade black. I held on to consciousness as best I could, knowing that I couldn't afford to pass out right now. If the three of us needed to get away again, I'd be a hindrance if unconscious. I dully noted a ripping noise and then felt a cloth being pressed against my wound. Pain flared through me and brought my mind back into sharp focus.

I looked at Mina, now in human form, as she continued to press down on my cut, blood soaking the cloth she had ripped from her shirt. Arizu hovered over her shoulder, worry plastered across her face.

I groaned and somehow managed to sit up, taking over putting pressure on my injury from Mina.

"Are we safe here for now?" I asked her. "I can keep going if we need to get away from here."

"No!" my cousin said forcefully. "We need to get you to a hospital before you bleed to death!"

It was then that I noticed how badly Arizu was shaking. And how many cuts she had received from the window shattering. Before I could comment on how she should worry about herself, Mina said, "Kaylon and Kiara should have the Corrupted all taken care of by now, so we can head back and get you both to a hospital." She shifted back into horse form. "I can carry you both, still." She knelt down like before as I tried to stand, but the loss of blood was too great and I almost passed out once again.

"Rox!" Arizu grabbed my good arm and helped me sit back down. "Don't worry," she said. "I'll lift you up onto Mina's back." I was about to give a sharp reply about not needing help getting atop the Horse Lyven, but found that I didn't have the energy to argue. After tying the ripped piece of cloth around my arm, my cousin helped me up and I clung to Mina's mane with the rest of my strength. Arizu sat behind me to help steady me, and then we started off at a brisk trot.

"I guess this is the reason I needed protection?" Arizu asked in a quiet voice, her arms clasped around my waist. I could still feel her shaking.

"Exactly," Mina replied.

"What even was that thing?"

The Horse Lyven was quiet for a moment before responding. "I know that I'm not supposed to tell you what the Corruption is, but I think it's alright to tell you what a Corrupted is. I mean, how can I not after it just attacked you? Corrupted are Lyvens who have succumbed to the Corruption. You've seen how it feeds off living organisms?" My cousin nodded. "Well, if it touches a Lyven's bare skin, the Corruption will immediately crawl into their pores, enter the bloodstream, make its way to the brain, and take control over that Lyven. After reaching the brain, it spreads over the skin as you saw, and the victim becomes a Corrupted. Sadly, the Lyven is killed during the process. The only thing we can do to get rid of a Corrupted is to completely destroy the body. That's why you saw my brother tear its leg off."

"But Kaylon bit it, and you kicked it," I pointed out skeptically. "Why aren't either of you Corrupted?"

"Kiara is a skilled biochemical engineer," came the

reply. "She's developed a cure for non-hosted Corruption and a vaccine that allows Lyvens to touch it without being Corrupted."

"Then why haven't you given this vaccine to everyone that you can?" Arizu asked, clearly disturbed about the whole situation.

"Unfortunately, the vaccine is unfathomably hard to make, and Kiara has only managed to produce four solutions of it in the years since she discovered how to create it. Me, my brother, our father, and Kiara are the only Lyvens who have been able to receive the vaccine." My cousin and I sat in silence as we processed this information.

"Thank you for telling us all of this," Arizu said. "I hope that you don't get in trouble with Kiara because you've said so much."

"Nah," Mina said. "She'll understand. And it's not like you weren't gonna find out sooner or later. I just think that this isn't something you need to wait for to be told. It's better you know now so that you don't become Corrupted. Since Kiara hasn't managed to produce a fifth solution of her vaccine yet, it's a very dangerous time for you."

"Why is it that the Corrupted came for *me*, though?" My cousin asked.

"Now, *that*, I can't tell you. Not because I'm not allowed to, but because I actually don't know." I felt Arizu slump in defeat behind me.

"I don't know why all of this is happening," she mumbled. "Why can't everything just be back to normal? And why am I all the sudden so important that I need protection from something I don't even fully understand? Why is it coming after me?" She laid her head against my back. "Roxlin, I'm sorry."

I turned my neck to look at her slumped figure. "Sorry for what? For not being told why you're targeted? For being targeted in the first place?"

Arizu didn't look up. She shook her head. "For being the reason you got hurt."

I gave a snort of derision. "Did you break a window and cut me with its broken pieces?" A hesitation, then another shake of the head. "Did you try to make me fall and hurt my shoulder worse?" Another shake of the head. "Did you try to hurt me or anyone else?" Arizu finally looked up at me, her face sad.

"No," she said.

"Then it wasn't your fault. Whatever this "Corruption" is, that's the thing to blame. Don't worry about me. I can take care of myself." I could tell that my cousin still blamed herself as she looked out at the passing landscape, but there wasn't much else I could say to comfort her.

I distracted Arizu by drawing her attention to different places we had passed on our race to the forest. Mina had traveled far in such a short amount of time, so distracting Arizu by pointing out the pretty gardens around houses, the many different Lyvens loitering around, and just weird things in general that I noticed helped pass the time it took to get back to Ulon's Ice Cream. Before long, we had stopped in front of the small building.

My wound had stopped bleeding by now, and I thankfully seemed to be doing fine. The pain from the wound still hurt like none other, but I didn't feel as lightheaded as before. I did wonder as to why I hadn't passed out from loss of blood or even just from the pain. Shrugging, I pushed the question away as I dismounted, accrediting it to me just being resilient.

The front of the shop didn't look all that different from before, despite the broken window. But we all knew to some extent the havoc that awaited us inside.

"Shouldn't we get to a hospital first?" Arizu asked Mina as we stood together at front of the shop.

Mina looked worriedly at Ulon's Ice Cream. She had changed into human form. "We do need to go there, but I was hoping to check on my brother first. Is that alright? Are both of you doing okay for now?"

We nodded, and the three of us headed inside.

Besides most of the furniture being completely destroyed, the Corrupted had been kind enough to leave the ice cream holders unmolested. The main destruction had consisted of the immediate room. Tiles and cement were torn up to show the bare earth beneath and giant cracks ran along the walls. Even amid the chaos, we spotted Kaylon and Kiara immediately.

They stood together talking quietly, facing away from us. They must have heard us come in, for they broke apart and greeted us as we approached.

"Did everything go alright?" Mina checked her brother over.

"Yeah," Kaylon replied as his sister inspected a cut above his eye. "Although, remind me to never bite one of those things again. They taste disgusting."

Mina continued to look over Kaylon as Kiara turned to Arizu and me. "Do you now see why it's important to guard your cousin?" She asked me.

I grudgingly nodded. "I see why. From what I gather, there are going to be plenty of more of them to come after her before whatever plan that *super-secret organization* of yours has comes into effect. But, *why aren't you telling us anything that's important?*" I hissed this last part with an added glare.

"Rox," Arizu used a hushed tone. "I think you're just wasting your breath. If they were going to tell us anything more, they would have done so way before now."

"She's right," Kiara said. "I don't have the authority to tell you. I'm just following my orders to keep quiet. Honestly, I think Arizu deserves an explanation, but again, not my call. The higher ups want to tell you about everything when you get to the palace."

I cocked my head, filing the information that Kiara wasn't the head of her group away in my brain. "Can you at least tell us who your superiors are?" I wasn't actually expecting her to say who. And I was right.

"Nope."

Arizu and I sighed in unison.

"It's time you two got yourselves healed," the Fox Lyven said as she turned away from us. "Mina, your brother is fine. Look over these girls."

The Horse Lyven looked surprised. "You mean I can show my ability to them?"

"There's no harm in it. So might as well fix them up here instead of having to go all the way to a hospital. You've already healed Kaylon all up anyways."

Now that she mentioned it, I noticed that the cut above Kaylon's eye was gone.

"Alright." Mina came over to us and went to take hold of my hand. I pulled away and glared at her.

She smiled. "Don't worry. My ability is that I can heal most wounds. I need to have direct contact with your skin, though. I'm actually the reason you didn't bleed to death on our escape to the forest, and why you didn't pass out after we stopped. It's quite a nasty wound you have there."

I continued to glare distrustfully, but held my hand out for Mina to take it. It was true that I should have at least passed out from loss of blood. Plus, it was better for me to make sure that her ability was really one of healing than it was for Arizu to have to be the first test subject. And it was true that Kaylon now seemed perfectly fine.

As soon as Mina took hold of my hand, the pain in my shoulder diminished. And after a few awkward minutes, the pain vanished along with any other cuts and bruises I'd had, including the bruise I'd received from my mother.

"That's amazing!" Arizu gushed. "Why aren't you working in a hospital? You could save so many lives!"

Mina blushed as she took Arizu's hand now. "Thank you. But I can actually only heal physical wounds. Mental disorders or sicknesses don't apply. And if I use my ability on too damaged of wounds, my ability will begin to drain me of life as a source to continue healing." Since Arizu's cuts were only minor, it didn't take as long as my shoulder wound to heal. After a brief moment, Mina released my cousin's hand.

"I understand," Arizu said with a large smile. "But that doesn't mean your ability is any less amazing! Look, I'm back in tip-top shape!" Arizu proceeded to start running around the room. She promptly tripped on a broken table and landed on her face.

"Oof. That looked like it hurt," Kaylon said with a laugh. I laughed as well, Mina and Kiara joining in. Arizu sat up and laughed as well, rubbing the side of her head where she had hit it.

When we had all quieted down, Kiara said, "It's time I leave. Like Roxlin noted earlier, more Corrupted will be showing up at any time, and it's my job to limit that number as much as I can." The short Fox Lyven looked at the twins and gestured to my cousin and me. "Take good care of these two, alright?"

Kaylon and Mina nodded as Kiara shifted to her Fox form and dashed away, leaping gracefully through the broken window as Mina had done not too long ago.

Chapter 9
Arizu

"So do we go back to your house now?" I asked Roxlin. She nodded. "Mother is getting more and more impatient. She thought that I'd be able to find you the same day she ordered me to. Of course, I wasn't really trying to find you because we were planning on meeting today." Roxlin sounded annoyed as she stated, "And hasn't this turned out to be an interesting day."

"It really has," Kaylon said. "It was actually the first time I've fought against a Corrupted. I've seen Kiara and Dad fight one, but Mina and I never have."

"You've obviously practiced a strategy concerning how you would protect Arizu, though," Roxlin said.

"That's right," Mina stated. "Kaylon distracts the enemy and I get her away from danger. Keeping her safe is our top priority." My cousin still looked skeptical at that statement.

"After all this we should at least trust them a little bit. They really did save our lives," I pointed out.

"That's true," Roxlin conceded grudgingly. "Ugh. This

whole thing is just such a mess." The Snake Lyven rubbed her temples.

"Tell me about it," I said with a smile. "But hey, our lives have just gotten more interesting! Kinda like we're characters in a book!" I stared thoughtfully at a cracked wall. "This whole situation actually kind of reminds me of that book called *Blood Ties* that I loaned to you, Roxlin."

Roxlin tipped her head. "You're right. It does resemble that book." She shook her head then, exasperated. "But a fictional book isn't important right now." My cousin turned to the twins. "So I assume you're still going to follow us around?"

"Yup," Kaylon said. "I do have to admit that it's pretty fun watching you guys do stuff." Roxlin's eyebrows drew together and she gave the Alligator Lyven a creeped-out look. He blushed. He must realized how his sentence had sounded. Mina closed her eyes in embarrassment.

"I'm sorry about my brother." She apologized to us. "He's a little socially awkward and doesn't always think before he speaks."

I laughed. "It's alright! I agree with him that it's fun to people watch, actually! I just don't usually watch people from outside their house." I teased him with a few pokes to his side. He blushed deeper, and I saw his eyes flick to Roxlin uncertainly, probably to see if she was still staring at him with her creeped-out expression. But my cousin only rolled her eyes, her face now relaxed.

I noted how Kaylon had seemed to care more about Roxlin's reaction to his remark than mine, and I gave a conniving smirk.

Roxlin noticed my smirk and glared suspiciously. "What's that smile for?"

"Oh, nothing," I replied nonchalantly. "But we should get going before it gets too late. You have to tell me about this ball we're all the sudden going to!" I turned to the twins. "Real quick, what's going to happen to Ulon's Ice Cream? Does it have to be disinfected or something?"

"No." Kaylon's blush had faded as he answered me. "The Corruption doesn't infect anything nonliving. Repairs will start whenever the owner wants them to begin."

I clapped happily. "That's good news! Well, I guess we'll see ya around. Have fun watching us!" I winked at Kaylon. He ducked his head and buried his face in his hands.

"Good-bye," Mina waved, laughing at her brother's reaction.

On our journey home, Roxlin told me what happened while I was gone. I was interested to learn about Selen and Kren, as well as them specifically requiring my presence at the palace.

"Do you think whoever tasked Kiara and her group to protect me is someone in the royal court? Someone who has control over Lyvens like those two?" I asked my cousin.

"It's quite possible and would make a lot of sense," she replied. "But I remember Selen having said that the monarchs themselves had personally invited our family to come. Kiara had said that everything will be explained to us at the palace, but Selen said he wouldn't have had our family come if he'd had a say in the matter. So I don't think they have a connection to her group. It would make sense if King Rolm and Queen Aulia knew about the Corruption, though. And it would make sense if they had a secret organization working for them to fix this strange problem that has popped up. . ."

We fell quiet. Kiara knew about us going to the palace, she had told us that we would be informed of what's going on when we arrived there, and the King and Queen personally requested our family to attend the ball. . . It was all too much of a coincidence to be a coincidence.

"Maybe we should just go with the flow and not worry about anything!" I suggested with a tense smile, my brain feeling overloaded from the revelation.

Roxlin raised an eyebrow. "How can we not worry when we literally just got attacked not more than two hours ago and have now figured out that the *freaking monarchs of Cillium* want something to do with you?"

I blinked at her. "By not thinking about it?"

Roxlin's lips tightened. "That's a great idea," she said sarcastically. "If we ignore them, all our problems will disappear."

"Exactly!" I said with a skip, mustering up all the enthusiasm I could.

Roxlin shook her head in exasperation.

Though she gave the appearance of disliking my idea of ignoring our problems, we didn't talk about our predicament anymore for the time being.

When we returned to Roxlin's mansion, Viern was waiting for us, sitting in a tall-backed leather chair in the living room.

I leaned over to Roxlin as we stood at the entrance of the room and whispered, "Has she been stalking us, too?" Roxlin gave a slight smile, but her attention was otherwise taken up by a staring contest between her and her mom.

"So, you finally decided to actually look for her." Aunt Viern said without any warmth of a welcoming parent. She hadn't even bothered to say hi to my cousin or me. "I know you hadn't been trying to find her before."

"Well, she's here now." The coldness of Roxlin's voice could have frozen a whole lake.

Geez, I thought. *Things have never been this tense between these two. I think the temperature has dropped a couple degrees.* While the staring contest continued, I shifted uncomfortably from foot to foot.

"You can leave and get packed up for our trip," my aunt said to me, not breaking eye contact with her daughter.

"Yes, Ma'am," I said, giving Roxlin an apologetic glance as I headed off. As soon as I turned the corner, however, I stopped and hid, wanting to hear the rest of the conversation.

"You've been very insolent lately, Roxlin," Viern said, her voice neutral. The neutrality seemed even more dangerous than if she had matched Roxlin's coldness.

"Forgive me, Mother." Sarcasm seethed in her words.

Viern sighed. "I hope you know, I honestly don't like violence." I heard movement and my body tensed. Viern must have stood up. "But I do believe it's sometimes a necessary evil to teach important lessons, such as respect." I heard a smack and almost sprang from my hiding spot from around the corner. I bit my lip to keep from growling. Tears collected in my eyes, and it wasn't from the pain of biting my lip.

I wanted to help Roxlin badly, but knew I'd just make things worse for the both of us if I tried to intervene. A second smack sounded, and I wrapped my arms around myself. My tears spilled over. I couldn't help but hate myself for standing idly by. However, Roxlin's strong voice made me freeze in shock.

"I let you hit me because, as my parent, it is your job to teach me. Even if your method for doing so is crappy. But I smacked you because I'm going to teach *you* a lesson now.

"I'm not a young girl who can be scared into submission anymore. I have my own thoughts and ideas, as well as my idea of right and wrong. Instead of suppressing my thoughts and feelings, you should learn to embrace my way of thinking and allow me to be myself."Footsteps were now coming right towards me. I took a gamble and stayed where I was, hoping it was Roxlin.

When she was the one who turned the corner, I sighed in relief and grabbed her into a hug. She stiffened from the unexpected action, but quickly relaxed when she realized it was me. And for the first time ever, she hugged me back.

We walked in silence back to our rooms, but before we parted to start packing, I said with my biggest smile, "I'm so proud of you, Rox. You were so brave!"

Roxlin smiled, her fanged grin solidifying the victory she had just won over her mom even as a purple bruise began spreading across her right cheekbone. "I figured that Mother wasn't as scary as facing down a seven-foot tall parasitic monster."

My smile dropped even as we celebrated for that brief moment. "Aren't you worried about what your mom might do in retaliation?" I worried now that the thought had entered my brain.

My cousin shrugged. "Not really. The worst she could do is beat me up or kill me. Either option I could deal with."

"If she did either of those things, you know I would fight

your mom 'till my last breath. So make sure neither actually happen." I grinned. "I don't want to die quite yet."

"It wouldn't even take these extreme circumstances to kill you. I'm pretty sure you'd accidentally trip and fall off a cliff even if walking on flat terrain.

"Anyways," Roxlin opened her bedroom door. "We'll be gone for a month, so pack accordingly." She went inside and closed the door, pride evident in her stride.

Despite worrying about retaliation from Aunt Viern, pride over Roxlin's accomplishment strengthened my own stride as well.

When I entered my own room, I realized that the duffle bag and backpack I had taken with me when I was kicked out had at some point gotten lost over the course of events that had occurred. I had plenty of clothes, but the ones in the duffle bag had been my favorites. . . I shrugged the unfortunate accident away.

Before I could even begin to search for a suitcase, however, a knock sounded on my door. I opened it and found Sou standing before me.

"Sou!" I was elated to see her.

Sou wrapped me in hug. Tears rolled down her caramel-colored skin. "I was so worried about you." She let me go and brushed her tears away. "Are you okay?"

I stepped away from the Bear Lyven and gave her a reassuring smile. "Of course I'm okay! It was easy-peasy being by myself in Avera!"

Sou wiped away a tear that I hadn't even realized had fallen from my eye. "Something tells me that you aren't really alright," she said with a tender look.

I hugged her again, tears falling harder. Gosh. I felt like *such* a cry-baby. "Trust me. I'm perfectly fine. It's just nice to know that someone other than Roxlin was worried about me. I honestly don't even know why I'm crying!"

"Oh, Honey. It's alright to cry. It helps heal the soul." Sou held me for a moment longer before letting go. She turned away to reach for something. "I wish I could stay longer, but I have chores to attend to," she said regretfully. "A friend told me to give these to you, though." She handed me my supposedly lost backpack and duffle bag as well as a suitcase.

I gaped at Sou, but before I could ask her any questions, she turned away and left me to my racing thoughts. The only Lyvens who would have known where my bags were would be Kiara's group. Sou was a part of this weird secret organization?! I could hardly believe it and contemplated chasing her down, but gave up the idea, knowing that I wouldn't get any answers from her. I sighed and just focused on packing. I would tell Roxlin about this new development later.

I didn't know exactly what I should take to the palace, but thought that it would be a good guess to bring formal clothes. I would have brought formal dresses if I'd had any. Unfortunately, I didn't really like looking for clothes, so I didn't have as many outfits to choose from as Roxlin. I sighed at the menial task of packing. The task bored me, and I already didn't like being alone right then. It gave me time to think, and nothing really made sense so thinking was just giving me a headache. I didn't like focusing on my problems, particularly the problems my cousin and I were wrapped up in. Doing so just made me feel confused and worried. And it didn't help that so many revelations had come to light today, creating more questions than answering previous ones.

I flopped onto my bed and tugged on my dingo ears in frustration. I hadn't even filled half my suitcase, but I needed a break – and some fresh air. I climbed out my window and wandered around the garden for a bit. The familiar sights, sounds, and smells didn't help, so I decided to take a walk around the block, hoping that less familiar scenery would distract my spinning mind.

I hadn't even gotten pass the second house that was settled next to my aunt and uncle's mansion when an unwelcome sight greeted me. Avo and her four other gang members were headed straight towards me. I saw Avo look around, presumably to see if Roxlin was with me. With nothing to stop her, she came right up to me and stuck her nose in my face. An unsettling feeling crept into my gut as she began to speak.

"Today must be my lucky day," she said gleefully. "Not only did I happen to run into you when I wasn't even trying to, your little *guard snake* isn't around to make stupid threats." Avo snapped her fingers and two of her friends immediately grabbed my arms and twisted them behind my back. One of the two kicked the back of my left knee which sent me to the ground in a kneeling position.

"Leave me alone, Avo," I growled. The bully pulled her arm back like she was gearing up to punch me square in the face.

"Oh, and why should I?" Avo wore a twisted grin, poised to strike. "This is payback as well as a warning to that disgusting snake that she shouldn't mess with me."

"I'm actually giving you a warning myself right now." I

heard my voice drop to an uncharacteristically dangerous degree, and the feeling in my gut hardened. "Let me go before you get hurt." A flicker of fear passed over Avo's face, but then arrogance settled across her features once again.

She waved her open hand at her friends, and they forced me onto both knees. "It's five of us against one of you. You're screwed." Avo threw her punch but, in that moment, the ominous feeling I had felt in my gut overtook me. And so it was that her blow never landed.

I lunged backward as Avo's arm swung towards my face. The kids holding my arms fell to the ground from the force of my movement. I broke free from their grasps as they hit and sprang up, the dark, unfamiliar feeling fueling my movements. Avo's two other bullies started toward me. I laid them out on the ground next to their fellow friends with a kick to the stomach of one and an uppercut to the jaw of the other. I knew Avo wouldn't have the guts to attack me alone, so I focused on bringing the two that had grabbed me down before turning my attention to the cowardly Cat Lyven. They had merely been knocked to the ground. Nothing more. So I kicked them each on the side of the head as they tried to get up. With them taken care of for the moment, I then quickly circled around so that Avo was in between me and her groaning lackeys.

"You should have heeded my warning," a voice that almost seemed not my own growled. I felt my canines enlarge as I shifted to my Dingo form. I vaguely realized in the back of my mind that I shouldn't have been able to do so right now. My shifting had never been successful in strenuous situations. Yet in seconds, I was fully transformed and leaped on top of the frozen girl, bringing her to the earth. She screamed in pain when I bit her neck. Blood splattered my face as I bit harder, my vision now blurred from the dark anger I felt and from the blood.

"Arizu!" A voice cried. It sounded familiar, but that wasn't important. The only important thing was killing this Lyven who had tormented me for so long.

"Arizu!" Came the cry again, desperation coating the voice. I felt hands tugging at me, trying to pry my jaws apart. But I wasn't letting go.

Suddenly, a sharp pain surged through my head, and my blurry vision turned black.

Chapter 10
Roxlin

I sat next to Arizu's bed in her room, worry darkening my gaze. My cousin lay quietly under the sheets, a too-still figure.

It had been over a week since Kaylon had been forced to knock her unconscious. Our family was supposed to have traveled to the palace that rested in Cillium's capital, Orthon, by then, but a doctor had strongly advised to not move Arizu until she had regained consciousness.

Kaylon stirred beside me in his chair from where he had been taking a nap. "You're still up?" he asked with concern in his voice.

I didn't look away from Arizu's prone body. "It's been too long, Kaylon," I said. "We've been able to get water down her throat, but she needs to eat. She's beginning to waste away like this."

"I'm sorry," Kaylon said for the umpteenth time. "If it wasn't for me, she wouldn't be like this."

I gave a tired sigh, "Kaylon, we've already gone over this so many times. If it wasn't for you, Avo would have died and

Arizu would have become a murderer. I don't think she could have lived with herself if she had killed someone. You pretty much saved her life. I'm just... I'm just still so confused as to why she attacked Avo like that in the first place. Arizu has no reservations in defending herself or others, but going to that extreme of a tactic..."

Kaylon leaned back in his chair, the violet moonlight that streamed through Arizu's open window glinting off his single earring. Ever since the accident, he had sneaked into my cousin's room through the window every night to check on her, obviously feeling guilty for the whole situation. Since I hardly ever left her side, I had told him that he didn't need to, but he did anyways. That meant we had spent a lot of time together over the week. Though I would have preferred to be by myself, Kaylon didn't talk much, so his company didn't bother me like another Lyven's might have.

Mina had even visited, but I didn't think she liked being near Arizu because the Horse Lyven felt powerless to help. Not like any of us didn't feel powerless as well. But she most likely felt even more useless because she had a healing ability, yet it only worked on physical wounds. She had gotten rid of the bump that had come from Kaylon's blow, but apparently, the thing that kept Arizu unconscious was a mental wound.

Suddenly, Arizu sat straight up and stared at the open window. Kaylon and I jumped as shock shot through me.

"Ari?" I asked tentatively, relief beginning to spread through my body. But I felt my blood run cold as my cousin started chanting in a flat, almost lifeless voice.

"*Blood ties to fate. Fate is tied to blood. My blood ties me to my fate. Blood ties to fate. Fate is tied to blood. My blood ties me to my fate. Blood ties to fate. Fate is tied to blood. My blood ties me to my fate. . ."* She continued to chant even after I grabbed her shoulders.

"Ari!" Panic made my voice rise. "Arizu!" No change. What was happening?! My cousin continued to chant. *"ARI!"* I screamed at her face, trying to get her to snap out of whatever had possessed her. She stopped.

"What the He-" Kaylon began. But he was cut off as Arizu grabbed my left arm in a painful grip. Her fingernails dug into my skin and I hissed in pain. Kaylon moved forward to try to help, but I stopped him with my free arm.

"Wait," I said through gritted teeth.

Arizu stared at me with glassed-over eyes, the light of life seeming to have disappeared from them. "You will betray me. Just like everyone else," she said in a coarse whisper. The Dingo Lyven then flopped onto her back, her eyes closed. Her face had a tormented twist to it, and she rolled around in her bed for a moment before finally falling still. Everything was now deathly silent.

I frantically rushed forward out of my seat and turned Arizu onto her back once again, feeling for the pulse in her neck. I clutched my heart in relief when I found one. I then sat back in my chair, tenderly touching my arm where Arizu had grabbed it. It was bruised, but nothing more. I would be fine.

"Are you okay?" Kaylon examined my arm.

"I'm fine." I was more concerned with what had just occurred. And in all reality, *what in this world had just occurred?* "Do you know anything about what just happened?" I asked

Kaylon, calming down now that the insane episode seemed to have passed.

He shook his head, his eyes wide in confusion. "I have no idea. No one ever informed me to look out for something like this. Mina's and my task has only ever been to keep Arizu safe."

I rubbed my temples in frustration. Nothing made sense anymore. I had all but given up on understanding the situation my cousin and I had been thrust into.

"I'd better inform Kiara about this new development." Kaylon stood up. I had to crane my neck to look at him from where I sat, since he was at least six feet tall. "If anything happens again, call for Mina immediately, alright?"

I snorted in derision. "I don't need Mina's help to take care of my cousin. As a matter of fact, I don't need yours, either."

Kaylon smiled at me, which irritated me to no ends. "I know. But it would make me feel better if you did. So will you?"

"I have no obligation to."

"That's why I'm asking."

"And why do I concern you so much? If I remember correctly, you're supposed to protect Arizu, not me."

Kaylon gave an exasperated sigh. "Just promise me, you stubborn snake."

"No," I replied, turning back to Arizu.

His arms wrapped around me and I stiffened. Though Kaylon was tall and skinny, he was quite strong. I tried to twist out of his embrace, but he gently held me tighter, trapping me against the back of my chair.

"I won't let go until you promise me," he whispered into my ear.

I turned my head to look at him, which left our faces very close together. "Get off me," I hissed, uncomfortable.

"Then promise."

I turned my head away. "Ugh. Fine. Now get away from me."

Kaylon laughed. Before I could punch him, he scampered away and leaped out the window. He sprinted away as I hurried after him. I stopped at the window sill and called angrily after him, "Next time I see you, I'm going to drop a spider down your shirt!" Then he was gone.

I touched my chest where my heart pounded, angry at Kaylon. But I was angrier at myself. And especially at this traitorous heart of mine.

"I knew it!" A familiar, happy voice said.

"Arizu?" I turned in surprise. My cousin sat up in her bed, a smile on her face. Her eyes were bright in the moonlight, not glazed over in the slightest anymore.

I approached her. "Are you okay?"

"Of course I am!" she replied. "Now, let's talk about what just happened between you and Kaylon." Her expression turned sly. "You know, you two are gonna end up together. I'm calling it."

"No," I said with a glare. " Kaylon was just being an idiot." I looked Arizu over. "Do you remember what you did just a few minutes ago?" I purposely changed the subject.

"Wasn't I sleeping?" Arizu cocked her head. "Did I do something weird while I was asleep?"

"No, it's nothing," I forced a smile. I decided that if she

didn't remember, it wasn't worth worrying her about it. "I'm just glad you're finally awake."

"How long have I been asleep?" The Dingo Lyven stretched her arms over her head and yawned.

"Eight days," I replied.

Arizu jumped out of bed. "*Eight days?*" she exclaimed in astonishment. "How could I be asleep for *eight days?*! What happened?" My cousin rubbed her temples. "Wait. . . I remember. . . I remember what happened now before I went unconscious." She looked at me, panic in her eyes. "Avo. Is she-?"

I shook my head before she finished her sentence. "It was a close call, but Kaylon stopped you in time. She made it."

Arizu let out a huge pent up breath of relief. "I'm so glad."

"Why did you bite Avo's neck, Ari?"

My cousin's face fell. "I don't. . . I don't know. Something came over me and I just. . . did it. It's like all the frustration I've felt over not having everything about our situation explained to us made me snap when Avo pushed my buttons."

"This is the first time something like this has ever happened, right? You've never done anything like this on Earth?"

"No, never. I'm always super careful when I'm over there." We were silent for a moment. "I'm scared, Rox," Arizu said quietly.

I furrowed my brows. "If you're worried about the Corruption, even though we don't know what Kiara's group has planned, I'm sure it will work to at least some extent. Plus, I'm here, and Mina and Kaylon are protecting you. So there's no reason to be."

My cousin shook her head. "Though the Corruption is

scary, for some reason, I'm not actually scared of it. No, what I'm scared of is. . . Myself. Rox, I still had control over myself. Sure, my vision became blurry and I did feel compelled by some weird force to attack. But I could have stopped. I could have stopped, yet I chose not to. I could have let go, but I didn't. . ." Arizu put her head in her hands. I wanted to say something to make her feel better, but words escaped me. All I could do was place a hand on her shoulder. Arizu was trembling badly. "Lyvens keep getting hurt because of me," she said in anguish.

I tightened my grip on her shoulder, finally finding something to say. "Stop it, Ari. You can't bottle up all the blame inside of you. You're going to tear yourself apart.

"But it's true!" She jerked away from my grasp. "Mina said that the Corrupted are targeting me. If you hadn't been next to me, you wouldn't have gotten hurt. Avo wouldn't have been nearly killed if it weren't for me. And Mina and Kaylon wouldn't be in danger if they weren't told to protect me." Arizu hunched more into herself. "You should stay away from me from now on, Rox."

After a moment of silence, I smacked my cousin upside the head. She looked at me in shock. "Shut it. Look, maybe you really are to blame. Does it look like I care? In my book, Avo got what she deserved. And in the case of me getting hurt, I chose to be around you, so it's at least partially my fault. And have you heard Mina or Kaylon complain about protecting you? No. You're scared of yourself? Well guess what. I'm not. I'm gonna stay by your side whether you like it or not." I held my cousin's stare, daring her to try to challenge me. She merely looked away.

Sighing, she climbed back into her bed. "I'm really tired all the sudden. I'm going to sleep. You should get some rest, too."

I pursed my lips in irritation at Arizu trying dodge her problems yet again. But it was true that it was late, and I hadn't slept well all week. Worrying about Arizu had kept me tossing and turning in bed

"Alright," I conceded. "Good night, then." I walked to the door and opened it.

"Roxlin?"

I turned around and looked at Arizu's dark form silhouetted against the moonlight. "Yes?"

"Thank you. For all that you do for me."

I snorted. "There's no need to thank me. I help you because I want to. Not because it's an obligation. Now, since you're now conscious, we'll probably be leaving for the palace tomorrow. Be prepared. Mother already hated having to delay our departure for so long." With that, I left Arizu's room and closed the door behind me. I slumped against the frame for a moment, thinking.

Kaylon's words from when we had met the second time rang in my ears. "*One of Arizu's deepest desires is to be free from emotional pain.*" That still worried me, even more so now. If Arizu continued to blame herself for everything bad that happened and would most likely happen, she was going to destroy herself.

I silently walked the short distance to my room, grateful that the events of the night hadn't awoken any of the inhabitants of the house. It would have been very bad if Mother had been roused. She had been on edge lately, probably due to the outburst of rebellion I had given her not so long ago.

I had felt so powerful then, so free when I had finally stood up to her. She'd done nothing in retaliation like Arizu had been afraid of, and she really just seemed uncomfortable around me now. Almost as if she didn't know what to say to me anymore. I didn't think Mother would all the sudden start treating Arizu and me with the respect we deserved, but, hopefully at least *something* in her attitude would change for the better.

I was already in my pajamas, so I climbed in bed as soon as I made it into my room. I felt drained after the weirdness of the night. My mind still didn't fully grasp what had occurred in my cousin's bedroom. Out of all the things that had happened to us, this was by far the creepiest. I didn't know what to think, let alone know if there was something I could do to help Arizu. Her chanting would've been enough to send most Lyven's packing, and with her saying that she'd still had control over herself when she'd attacked Avo. . . It gave me chills.

It was hard to believe, though. Arizu was always so gentle, only fighting when absolutely necessary. The only way it made sense was that Arizu had only *thought* that she was still in control. In actuality, the thing that she claimed had "compelled" her had really taken over her body. I didn't know which explanation disturbed me more.

With these troublesome thoughts in mind, I drifted off into a fitful sleep.

Chapter 11
Arizu

Despite having said I was tired, I could only stare blankly at the ceiling after Roxlin left my room.

It was true I didn't remember doing anything while I was unconscious as Roxlin had mentioned, but I remembered the nightmare I'd had vividly.

In my nightmare, there was a single Lyven standing next to me in a dark room. There was only one bright light that lit the surroundings. It was blue/white and came from a thing that resembled the Gate I used to travel between Cillium and Earth. I turned to the Lyven. Though I couldn't hear any sounds or words spoken between us, I could tell that I trusted him. I also knew that I feared that blue/white Gate like no other thing. I reached out for the Lyven, and he took my hand. I began to turn away from the Gate, but I could feel confusion as my companion tugged me back around. I tilted my head in question. I saw his lips move, and felt panic begin to set in. The one I felt I could trust above anyone else then kissed me gently, picked me up, and tossed me into the blue/white light.

The last thing I felt was immense pain and betrayal. And the only thing I heard was the whispered words, *"Blood ties to fate. Fate is tied to blood. My blood ties me to my fate"* before I awoke to Roxlin and Kaylon talking.

Both of them had been too busy to notice me wake up, which I was grateful for. I didn't want to worry either of them, and was able to compose myself by the time Kaylon left.

After wondering what my nightmare had meant for at least an hour, I was finally able to fall asleep. When I awoke to the light streaming in from my still open window, I felt bone-dead tired instead of refreshed. I contemplated going back to sleep, but knew I needed to pack the rest of my bags so that I could be ready to leave for Orthon. I really didn't want Viern to get angrier at me.

I had just zipped my final bag up when a knock sounded at my door. I opened it to see Sou and Roxlin standing there.

"Hi!" I said brightly. I had by now pushed all my tiredness and worries to the side and was now focused only on the excitement of going to the palace. Not every Lyven got to visit the palace, and most certainly not very many got invited to a royal ball.

"Good morning!" Sou replied as Roxlin gave a *harrumph* in response. My guess of Roxlin's bad mood was that she hadn't slept well the night before.

"We leave after lunch," Roxlin said.

Grinning, I replied with a happy, "Alright!"

Roxlin headed off towards her room without a good-bye.

Man, she must really *have not slept well*, I thought with a chuckle. Sou, however, lingered, and I turned my attention to her.

"Can I help you?"

Sou looked at me warmly. "Kiara told me to give you a heads up that Mina will be tagging along on our ride to the palace."

I tipped my head. I wasn't expecting to hear that. "How did you manage to get that by Viern?"

"Since I'm coming to the palace as well to be a handmaid for Viern, I told her that it would be nice to have help. I'm playing Mina off as a family relation of mine who will help with my duties."

I smiled. "That's so cool! But what about Kaylon?"

"He'll be meeting us there."

"Works for me! Anything else?"

Sou wrapped me in a hug and then began walking away down the corridor. "Lunch is in thirty minutes. Don't be late!"

I waved good-bye and then shut my door on the Bear Lyven's retreating back, feeling weirdly okay with Sou being apart of Kiara's group. It seemed right, seeing as the only Lyven's who had ever treated me like an actual living creature after knowing about my heritage were those of the Fox Lyven's group. Besides Roxlin, of course.

I idled the rest of my free time away reading in my room, hopping up and going immediately to the dining room when called.

It was a simple, quiet lunch. Almost no words were spoken, especially between Roxlin and her parents. It seemed almost as though there was a ticking bomb about to go off, but nothing ever happened. I was finally able to relax only when we began loading our luggage out to two sleek white porths, which was the name of the vehicles most High-Class

Lyven's chose as their mode of transportation. Viern's two porths were the equivalent of limos on Earth.

I greeted Mina happily when she arrived, and when everything was loaded, all three of us girls climbed into one porth while Roxlin's parents and Sou climbed into the other.

It was very roomy inside our porth, with plush seats and a lot of space to move around. Snacks were loaded around the space in small compartments. I quickly sniffed out my favorites of the snacks and began chomping down.

"We literally just ate not more than an hour ago," Roxlin said to me while I stuffed my face full.

"So?" I mumbled with a full mouth. Roxlin raised an eyebrow but said no more as she leaned back in her seat. After a moment, I heard her breathing turn deep and regular. I guessed that her probable rough night had caught up to her.

"Want a snack?" I asked Mina in a quieter tone of voice. Roxlin was normally a light sleeper, so as she slept I would usually talk as quietly as possible or avoid talking altogether. But I knew from past experiences that when she slept during the daytime, she wasn't waking up unless an explosion went off next to her ear. So just a slightly toned-down speech was good.

The Horse Lyven apparently didn't realize that Roxlin was asleep, however, and replied in her usual tone, "Sure. What do you have?"

As I showed her the options, I glanced at my sleeping cousin. Just as expected, she was still asleep. Since the Snake Lyven had no eyelids, it looked like she was just staring blankly at the interior of the porth. It was creepy to anyone not used to it.

Mina turned to Roxlin and offered her a bag of snacks. "Want some?"

I held back laughter as Mina sat there for a moment, snacks held out. Roxlin, of course, didn't answer. I quickly composed myself when she turned to look at me questioningly. An idea popped into my head, and it took much self-control to not let a sly smile slip across my face.

In a regular tone of voice, I said, "Roxlin is in a bad mood. But you know what will cheer her up?" Mina tipped her head to the side. "Hearing about your life!" My friend looked skeptical. I continued, "I know it doesn't seem as though she would like hearing about peoples' lives, but trust me. She loves listening to people talk. It's why she's so quiet! So go ahead and start telling her stories about yourself."

Mina still looked unsure, but seemed to decide to trust me. She began telling the sleeping Snake Lyven about her life.

After about two minutes into Mina's first story, Roxlin let out a soft snore, and I couldn't hold my laughter any longer. Mina looked so confused. It was priceless. Through gasps of breath I said, "Roxlin - *gasp* has been - *gasp* asleep - *gasp* this whole - *gasp* time!" *gasp*

Mina glared at me. "Are you kidding me? You've been letting me talk to a sleeping Lyven this entire time?" I nodded, trying to catch my breath.

"It's not that funny!" she snapped, clearly ruffled because of me laughing at her.

"I'm sorry! I'm sorry!" I waved my hand at her in a dismissive manner, my laughter dying down. "I'm sorry. I just couldn't help myself!" Mina huffed and looked out the window. After a moment, I pulled a snack from one of the compartments, opened it, and waved it under Mina's nose.

"Will you accept more food as an apology?"

Mina looked at me and then grinned. "Yeah, I guess that will do."

The rest of the eight hour drive was uneventful. Roxlin slept most of the way, only waking up a few hours before our destination. Mina and I had some nice conversations, but even I drifted off at some point.

It was dark when we finally pulled up to the gates of the palace. Lights lit up beautiful emerald grass and plants of all kind decorated the grounds. The assortment of plants created a kind of seemingly wild atmosphere, though it was obvious everything was precisely where it was supposed to be. Lights also shone upon the palace even as brilliant lights shone from within. And boy was the palace quite a spectacle to be seen. Even more so than the grounds that surrounded it.

The tall, dark gates opened onto a smooth paved pathway that led to the enormous structure. Being the oldest building in the Lyvens' recorded history, it was an older style, castle-looking edifice. Turrets stood majestically next to tall spires, and the red stone the palace was built from made it look as though it was bathed in blood.

Mina didn't seem as awe inspired as both Roxlin and I, but she did stare at the building with pride. "Kaylon and I grew up in the palace, you know," she told us cousins.

I looked at her in excitement. "Really? Oh my gosh that's so cool! How was it like growing up in such a place?"

The Horse Lyven stared thoughtfully out the window as we got closer to our destination. "Well, there were a lot of things to do. There are tons of hidden passages that Kaylon and I liked to explore. Another thing is that the palace is always busy with many people constantly coming and going. A quiet day never passes here. A place this large and old also needs a lot of upkeep, as well as improvements. So combined with our knowledge of the secret passageways, Kaylon and I were always able to eavesdrop on many different adults without them noticing. That's actually the reason we ended up being apart of our father's group. We listened in on a few of his meetings, and by the time he found out what we had done, we knew too much. So our dad let us join when he thought we were old enough."

I listened intently to Mina's tale while taking in every sight I could. Everything there was even more beautiful than Avera, which was hard to believe. But it was true, and I wanted to commit every little detail to memory.

The two porths pulled up to and parked before the the main doors of the palace. The large, thick, metal doors swung open as our group began to climb out of our respective vehicles. Four men dressed in ceremonial, military looking outfits greeted us. One I recognized immediately.

Kaylon smiled at Mina, Roxlin, and me as Roxlin leaned over to me and whispered, "You see those two Lyvens?" She gestured subtly at the two head Lyvens. Both were tall and imposing, but the dark-skinned Leopard Lyven had a gentle smile on his face whereas the Eagle Lyven wore a disapproving frown.

"Yeah," I said, wondering why the two looked familiar.

"Those are the Lyvens who came to inspect our family to see if we were worthy to be invited to the ball."

The memory of passing the two Lyvens on our way into her mansion right before I bit Viern flashed through my mind. "Ooooooh, I see," I whispered back. "Cool!"

"Welcome," the Eagle Lyven said dryly. "I see you were so gracious as to only be five days late. I was afraid you would arrive here when you were supposed to and require us to scramble to have things ready for you." The sarcasm in his voice was even more than I usually heard in Roxlin's voice. It was impressive.

"As I informed you before," Viern hissed in disdain, "There was an unexpected circumstance that demanded our delayed departure."

"Yes, yes. So I heard." The Eagle Lyven's eyes flicked to me and softened. I stared back in wonder. Was he also a part of the secret organization? Did he know why I was required to be here? But he seemed like the one Roxlin had said didn't want our family to be invited. So what was the deal?

The Leopard Lyven stepped forward. "Forgive my partner's rudeness. We're so very glad you all made it here safe and sound. We will now show you to your rooms. But don't worry about your luggage; it will be delivered to you shortly."

With that, we then split into four groups. The Eagle Lyven took Sou to where she would be staying, the Leopard Lyven took Roxlin's parents to their room, and Mina headed off with the last Lyven that had come to greet us. I noticed that the man had horse ears atop his head. Could that have been Kaylon's and Mina's father?

With the departure of Mina and the other Horse Lyven, that left Kaylon to guide Roxlin and me to our rooms.

Kaylon bowed mockingly to us as we began to head off.

"Welcome to this humble abode." He glanced at Roxlin. "I thought you said you were going to drop a spider down my shirt the next time you saw me, though?" He teased.

"Oh, you're right. I did say that. Sorry. You're just such an easy Lyven to forget about, it completely slipped my mind."

Kaylon grinned and then turned to me. "How are you feeling?"

"Good," I replied. I then beamed at him. "Thank you so much for stopping me from killing Avo, by the way! You're literally a life saver."

He laughed nervously. "Heh, well, I mean, I'm sorry-"

I cut him off. "Nope! No being sorry! It's over and done with, and you did the right thing." Kaylon ran a hand through his hair, still looking unsure of himself.

"Told you," Roxlin mumbled under her breath.

I proceeded to slap Kaylon on the back. "I won't hold it against you, so don't hold it against yourself."

As we passed the front doors and entered into the interior of the palace, I froze in place, gawking at the sight. "Holy crap. . ."

Chapter 12
Roxlin

"Holy crap" was right. The inside of the palace was magnificent, deserving every awe-inspired title Arizu and I could have come up with. The roof was a stained-glass dome of artistic mastery. Different sections depicted prominent scenes of Cillium's history in breathtaking beauty. A golden carpet ran across the red stone and continued up a grand staircase. More stained glass fit neatly between narrow windows that rested high along the walls, and a large, golden chandelier hung from the middle of the dome.

"This is amazing," I said, awestruck. "You and Mina grew up here?" I asked Kaylon.

The Alligator Lyven looked around with the same pride as his sister. "Yep! All seventeen years."

Arizu was trying to stare at everything all at once as Kaylon led us onward up the grand staircase. Her brown eyes were wide and her mouth hung open. "I have never seen anything like this in my entire life," she said. "Kaylon, you *have* to show us more of the palace. Especially some of those secret passages Mina told us about."

Kaylon ran a hand through his hair. "Uh, I don't think that's a good idea. I can show you more of the palace, sure. But a lot of the passages have been found and blocked, and all of them were pretty small. Plus, it'd look suspicious for guests to be found around the places where a lot of them are located."

"Oh *please?*" she begged. "I want to see more of the palace!" Kaylon still looked about to refuse, but Arizu really wanted to see more of the wonders this place held, so I said, "Just taking a peek wouldn't hurt anything as long as you were with us, right?"

He still looked about to protest, but then sighed with a defeated smile. "You two just had to gang up on me. Alright then, fine. But if you're called out for being suspicious, don't say I didn't warn you."

"Yay! Thank you!" Arizu jumped up and down.

Arizu and I continued to gawk at all the wonderful decorations, art, and architecture as we were led to our rooms. By the time we arrived, we were worn out from just having taken in only a small portion of the palace. It didn't help that it was late as well.

"Kiara made sure to arrange it so that your rooms were right next to each other." Kaylon gestured to the two guest bedrooms.

"Speaking of Kiara," Arizu began. "Will she finally tell us what's going on now that we're here?"

"She won't, but our superiors will."

"There's no need for you to refer to them only as your superiors," I said flatly. "Arizu and I already figured out who they are."

Kaylon started. "Are you serious? How did you figure it out?"

I shrugged. "Kiara actually gave us a lot of clues to work with, as well as that Eagle Lyven named Selen." The Alligator Lyven looked shocked. "Oh, wipe that look off your face," I said irritably. "We aren't stupid enough not to connect the dots from the information we've gathered, even with how much you secret organization Lyvens try to keep us in the dark. Now, when will the King and Queen finally tell us what's going on?"

"Well...Whenever they deem it proper," Kaylon replied simply.

Arizu growled in frustration. Even her patience was probably wearing down to the bare minimum. Mine was already gone, and I'm sure my face showed it.

Kaylon looked at us apologetically. "I'm sorry. I honestly don't know when they'll tell you." My cousin and I sighed in unison.

"Are we allowed to look around the palace by ourselves while we wait for both the ball and an explanation, at least?" Arizu wondered.

"Well, like I said earlier, it might seem suspicious if you two just wander around..." Kaylon's eyes lit up with an idea. "The palace actually has an amazing library that's open to the public! You guys could spend some time there."

"And of course you know that we both enjoy to read since you've creepily watched us from behind bushes, yes?" I asked dryly.

Kaylon's face turned bright red. "I, uh, well..."

Arizu laughed, her frustration seemingly gone. "The

library sounds great! Roxlin and I will probably check it out tomorrow. And don't forget that you're supposed to show us some of those secret passages!"

While the color of his face calmed down a bit, Kaylon told us how to get to the library and then bid us good night. Arizu and I said good night as well and then entered our respective rooms.

The guest room I was given was even nicer than my room at home. It was a large, square space with a bathroom to the left of the entry. A big four-poster bed sat pushed against the farthest red stone wall with a vanity to the right of it. A wardrobe rested close to the vanity. My luggage had been placed beside it. A few smaller paintings than what my cousin and I had passed hung around the room, and a golden carpet continued the theme of the palace entry. A desk sat along the right wall, and a glass door to the far right of the back wall led out to a balcony that I assumed looked out over more beautiful gardens.

There was still around two weeks until the ball, so I decided to unpack the contents of my suitcase into the wardrobe. No sense in having to live out of my suitcase for all that time.

Once finished, I slipped into my pajamas and went to the bathroom to get ready for bed. It didn't take long, and I was soon able to turn out the lights and climb in bed. The mattress was super plush, almost to an uncomfortable point. But I was still tired despite my long nap, and fell quickly asleep.

Light streaming into my room from the balcony door awoke me. I slid out of bed and stretched, feeling well rested. I went about my usual daily routine as if I were back home, and soon left my room to see if Arizu was ready for the day.

After my cousin answered my knocks, I saw that she was still in her pajamas and looked completely disheveled.

"Woah," I said. "What happened to you during the night?"

Arizu smiled brightly as if she was trying to compensate for how weary she looked. "Oh, don't mind me!" she laughed. "I just didn't sleep well. Probably because of being in a new place and because of all the excitement of seeing the palace."

They were believable explanations, but something seemed off with the Dingo Lyven this morning. However, I knew that if I asked she would just brush it aside, so I merely said, "Hurry and get ready. I'm not sure what we're supposed to do for breakfast, but if we have to go somewhere, I don't want to have to walk around with you looking like that." I gave Arizu a smirk as she nodded and began scampering quickly about, trying to get ready in a decent amount of time.

I closed the door behind me as I entered her room. Hers was identical to mine but in mirror image. The bathroom was on the right side, the desk was on the left, and the door leading to her balcony was along the back wall on the far left.

"How do you like this room?" I asked Arizu as I sat on her messy bed to wait.

"I like it!" she replied as she continued to rush around. She then promptly went into the bathroom and closed the door.

I leaned back, bored, but then sat up as I felt the pace of familiar footsteps coming towards the door. A knock soon came, and I hopped off the bed to answer. "Hey, Sou." I was happy to see her.

"Good morning, young Master," the Bear Lyven said with a warm smile. "How are you this morning?"

"Good. What about you?"

"I'm doing perfectly fine, thank you." Sou held a silver platter out to me. "This is your breakfast, courtesy of the palace kitchens."

I took the platter from her and looked at its contents. The main plate seemed to contain a crepe of some sort, fresh fruit was held in a bowl next to it, and silverware rested on a napkin beside the food. Sou poured a glass of milk and set it in a holder beside the rest of the breakfast.

"Thank you," I said to Bear Lyven.

"My pleasure." She nodded to me and then pushed her cart towards the other guest room.

"Oh, actually," I called to her, stopping her before she took more than two steps. "This is Arizu's room. I was just waiting in here for her to get ready."

I set my meal down on the desk as Sou got Arizu's platter ready. She then handed it to me and said, "I wish I could stay longer and visit with you girls, but I have to get to my other duties."

"It's okay. I understand."

Arizu finally came out of the bathroom. "Sou!" she exclaimed happily. She ran forward and gave the Bear Lyven a hug. "What are you doing here?"

"She came to give us breakfast," I answered, holding her platter up.

"Oh awesome! Thank you!" my cousin said to Sou.

"Of course," Sou said, letting go of Arizu and taking hold of the food trolley. "Sorry that I have to run, but enjoy your breakfast, and hopefully we can talk later today."

"Alright!" Arizu said with a wave. "Bye!" She shut the door as I carried her food over and placed it next to mine on the desk.

We ate our breakfast quickly, agreeing to visit the library Kaylon had told us about afterwards. We left the empty plates on the desk and headed there in companionable silence.

After only getting lost about two times and having to ask a few palace workers where the library was, we finally made it. Hopefully it would be worth the trouble to find.

Besides being large, being about an entire fourth of my house, and having books crammed close together on every inch of shelves that reached all the way to the ceiling, the library was pretty unremarkable. A Mouse Lyven who sat behind a large desk greeted Arizu and I with a smile. "Hello," she said to us. "Looking for a specific book?"

I shook my head. "No, we're just browsing."

"Okay, then. Just so you know, fiction is to the left of me, and non-fiction is to the right." She pointed in the respective directions. Arizu and I separated without another word, her going to the fiction side and me going to the non-fiction side. After looking around for a bit, I picked a book out about the monarchy of Cillium, opened up to a random page, and began to read.

Unlike monarchies of the past, the eldest child of the King and Queen does not take power. The strongest, most powerful, and most capable child, chosen by the King and Queen, does.

Once ascended to the throne, the King or Queen, along with their spouse, are no longer tied to only one animal form. They take upon the mantle of every animal, becoming able to take whichever form they please. This enhances their power to unimaginable heights. Though, and not always unfortunately, they are still susceptible to death by natural causes or by a well placed sword.

Not everything is known about the power of the Kings and Queens of Cillium. Much of their power is a closely guarded secret passed down between the monarchs. However, one thing is known for certain. Only those of the current bloodline are able to receive the power and forms of all animals. A very complicated rite can be used to switch the royal bloodline to another, but no known source has this rite recorded...

After a while of reading, I got bored of the book and, after putting it back in its proper place, began looking for a new book. Going to the far back of the non-fiction space, I found many old and large volumes of Cillium's recorded history. I was about to leave and visit the fiction side where Arizu was when a red leather-bound book with gold lettering caught my attention. It was a lot smaller than the books around it, and it looked really familiar. Before pulling it out, I read the title on its spine. I felt my breath catch.

No way... I was shocked. *This has to be a mistake. There's no way this book could be here.* Especially *in the non-fiction part of the library.* Yet, there was no indication of any other book not being in its proper place. There wasn't even any dust on any of the thousands of books I could see. So for this specific book out of all the thousands to have been misplaced here. . . It was just highly unlikely. But, that had to be the case. Because there was no way that the book Arizu had given me awhile ago to read could be non-fictional. And for me to find it among the records of Cillium's history on top of everything?

I pulled the book from its place and stared at the gold lettering. The two words of its title, *Blood Ties*, seemed to stare right back at me.

Chapter 13
Arizu

I was surprised when I heard Roxlin frantically calling out my name. It wasn't like her at all, so I knew something highly abnormal must have happened. I found her in one of the aisles with a red, leather-bound book held tightly in her hands. Agitation was written across her face.

"Rox, what's wrong?" I asked worriedly.

She shoved the book into my hands. "Look at this," she replied abruptly. I stared at the cover for a moment and almost dropped the book in shock when I read the title.

Blood Ties was a book my father had given me for my birthday last year. This wasn't an exact replica of the book - mine had been a regular hardback and the title was a different font. But I thought that *Blood Ties* was just a normal fantasy book my father found on Earth to give me. What was it doing here?

"I found this in the history section on the non-fiction side. And look at how it's written." I did as Roxlin said and opened the book, quickly scanning through the pages. The story seemed to be the same, but it was written in first person and seemed to be a journal of sorts. And the mythical creatures that had been in my version of the book? They were replaced with the name of Roxlin's and my species. The main "characters" were now Lyvens, and the name of the evil they had to fight against was changed to. . . The Corruption. My mind went numb.

I handed the book back to Roxlin and began pacing back and forth across the aisle, tugging at my furry ears in anxiety.

"Roxlin, I don't know how many more insane developments I can handle. I feel like I'm about to explode. *WHAT IS GOING ON?!*" I screamed this last part, not caring who was around to hear me. I collapsed to my knees.

I had managed to play off another nightmare that I'd had last night, but between what I did to Avo, the nightmares, being attacked by a Corrupted, and being left in the dark about my predicament. . . This new addition was about to break me.

"Ari, calm down." Roxlin knelt down beside me.

I looked at her, feeling like I was going to throw up. "*Calm down? How can I calm down?! Why are they doing this to us? What's the point in leaving us in the dark? What does any of this mean?!*" I recognized my voice as how it had sounded right before I almost killed Avo. My vision turned blurry, and I had to begin fighting down the urge that now arose inside of me to tear something apart. I shut my eyes tight. My breath came in gasps.

Roxlin began rubbing my back soothingly, trying to calm me down. "Deep breaths, Ari. Focus on your breathing," Roxlin said, her voice strained.

After a few tense minutes of following her advice, I

managed to get my breathing under control, and my dark urge left me. I fell back against the bookshelf behind me, feeling drained of all energy. My vision was clear when I reopened my eyes, and I was able to think more rationally. "I'm so sorry, Rox. I don't understand why I reacted this way. Please, forget what just happened." I didn't look at my cousin for fear of the expression I would find on her face.

What must Roxlin think of me? I wondered ruefully. *She must think I've finally gone insane.*

After several minutes of silence, I smiled weakly at the ground. "Let's see what we can figure out about this book. So, maybe. . . My mom revised the version of *Blood Ties* I own? Or, more likely, maybe Grandma Paryle and Grandpa Jaspes revised it and gave it to my dad to give me?" A sudden thought struck me. Mother freaking- why hadn't I thought of this before we had left her house? I could have quickly gone through the Gate to Earth and asked our grandparents!

I looked at my cousin with wide eyes. "What if our grandparents know what's going on? Remember how I said our situation seemed similar to the one in *Blood Ties*? Maybe this whole Corruption thing has happened before and they wanted me to have a version of this book as a sort of warning! Dang it, they could have probably shed some light on our situation!" I mentally kicked myself for not thinking of them having information sooner. But it was too late. Roxlin and I couldn't visit them now.

"We don't know if they would have actually known anything," Roxlin pointed out.

"Well, it couldn't have been my mom. She died during childbirth. And my dad is human. He doesn't know anything about the Lyvens, let alone enough to know about this book and know to revise it so that I wouldn't find it suspicious. It *must* have been our grandparents."

Just then, the Mouse Lyven that had greeted us at the entry of the library came around the corner, hiding behind a familiar figure.

The handsome Leopard Lyven that had welcomed our family to the palace looked at us in concern as the Mouse Lyven peeked around his tall figure.

He spoke in a deep, rumbling voice. "Yalet said she heard a scream come from this direction. Is everything alright?" I may have been good at coming up with excuses, but as Roxlin had once said, I usually never lie. So all I could do was stare up at the imposing Lyven from where I sat on the floor, trying to come up with a plausible reason as to why I would have screamed. Thankfully, Roxlin *was* good at lying.

"Everything's alright, Sir," she said smoothly. "My cousin just banged her elbow on one of the bookshelves. Nothing serious."

"It sounded like someone was getting murdered, though!" the Mouse Lyven said with panic in her voice.

"Does it look like anyone was murdered here, Ma'am?" Roxlin asked her. The librarian slowly shook her head. "Well, then there you go."

"As long as you say everything's alright, I believe you," the Leopard Lyven said. "Yalet, you can go back to your desk now. Thank you for coming and getting me. I was actually searching for these two anyways." The Lyven named Yalet looked at the Leopard Lyven in admiration and nodded, quickly scampering back down the aisle to her desk.

The handsome Lyven faced my cousin and me. "I don't think we've met." He held one large hand out to help me up. I took the proffered hand, and he hoisted me easily to my feet. He did the same to Roxlin. "My name is Kren. I had the pleasure of meeting Roxlin a while back when I was sent to evaluate her family."

"So I heard!" I put enthusiasm into my voice even though I felt none. "My name's Arizu. You said you were searching for Rox and me?"

Kren nodded. "I was told to inform you that dresses will be made for you two for the ball. Your measurements need to be taken today if the dresses are to be completed on time. I'm here to take you to the seamstresses."

Well, that was neat. I definitely hadn't expected something like that to come about. Though, I was learning that there was no use in having expectations for the future. Everything you predicted was just going to go up in flames anyways.

Kren's eyes flicked to the book *Blood Ties* that was still held in Roxlin's grip. "Interesting looking book you have there. What's it about?"

Roxlin was really good at keeping her facial expressions under control, so I instinctively knew to watch her body language instead of her face when she was asked a question. So even though she wore a perfect mask of indifference, I saw her posture stiffen. "Oh, it's a fictional romance novel about a man who kills someone in order to protect his lover. The lady waits for him until he gets out of prison even though she has many suitors who chase after her."

Kren turned away and began leading Roxlin and me

back out of the library. "You didn't strike me as a romantic, Roxlin," he said with an easy grin.

"Well, that's the funny thing about only meeting someone twice. You don't suddenly know everything about that Lyven."

The Leopard Lyven laughed, his white teeth flashing against his dark skin. "You have a point there."

Roxlin checked *Blood Ties* out from the library, and then Kren led us to where we would be getting measured for our dresses.

When we were finished with the seamstresses, we were told by a messenger that lunch was ready. We were led to a grand dining hall where we had lunch with Sou, Roxlin's parents, and Mina. When that *excruciatingly* awkward meal was *finally* over, Roxlin and I made it to her room, and I was able to ask her why she had lied to Kren. "He seems like an good Lyven," I said to her. "So why?"

"We don't know if he's part of Kiara's group. Freaking, we don't even actually know if we can trust Kiara's group even if he is. I really think that this book holds a lot of clues as to what's going on. So the fewer Lyvens who know about it, the better. And, well," my cousin hesitated, then continued, "I felt something weird when he asked me about the book. I can't explain it completely, but it felt kind of like. . . dread?"

I pulled on my ears and sighed. "Rox, I feel really worn out. I don't want to think about anything anymore. I'm just gonna call it an early night and hit the hay, alright?"

"It's barely afternoon, though."

"I know." We stared at each other for a moment before Roxlin finally looked away.

"Alright. Come get me if you need anything."

When I got to my room, I immediately went to my balcony door and opened it, letting crisp, cool air into my room. The fresh air made me feel better after the ordeal of this morning. Despite actually being tired, it had been too long since I was outside. I was feeling cooped up.

Walking out onto my balcony, I looked over the railing, seeing if I could drop down easily to the gardens below. The second floor where my room was stationed was too far up, so I looked for an alternate route down. I noticed that the red stone of the palace were large blocks with fairly decent cracks between each one. Being not the smartest person on either Earth nor Cillium, I decided to try to climb down the wall of the palace. It would have, of course, made more sense to leave my room and find an exit out to the gardens, but I didn't want to risk Roxlin hearing me leave after I had said I was going to sleep.

Everything was going well, and I had almost made it to the ground.

"I didn't realize we had a Spider Lyven staying here," a voice surprised me.

I started, and my fingers slipped from between the blocks of red stone. I landed on the ground, hard.

As I laid in the grass, winded, a boy around my age peered at me from where he stood. He was darker skinned than the Leopard Lyven Kren, with piercing blue eyes and slicked-back, black hair. His hair looked so gelled, I wouldn't have been surprised if he had used an entire bottle of the stuff to keep his hair permanently in place.

"You know," I said as I sat up. "You could have caught me

or at least somehow broken my fall. Since, well, you *were* the cause of it."

The boy stared at me with a stern expression. When he spoke, I noticed that his voice held a slight accent. "Is it really my fault if you were the one dangerously climbing down the wall?"

I leaned my back against the red stone, feeling a little angry at this kid's lack of an apology. I studied him more closely.

He wore a fitted red suit and stood with a straight posture, looking proud, if not a little arrogant. He was shorter than Kaylon and slightly stockier. And, I had to admit, was pretty good-looking to boot. A pair of wolf ears flicked in what seemed like annoyance. As if he were the one with any right to be annoyed.

I wished, not for the first time, that I had an ability of my own to use on him. Something like Roxlin's, where I could have the advantage of knowing what one of his deepest fears was. But nope. I was left to fend for myself using only my wit. Which, being honest, wasn't one of my strongest points.

"If you startle a squirrel as it climbs and it falls, is it the squirrel's fault for you startling it?" I asked the boy in response to his lame argument.

The Wolf Lyven cocked his head. "That was a better response than what I thought you would give. But, it still stands that you aren't a squirrel. Therefore, your argument is complete . . ."

"Finish that sentence, and you won't have a tongue to use anymore." I smiled after I cut him off, not in the mood to be looked down on.

The boy paused, seemingly taken aback by my sharpness. "Threaten me again, and you won't have a place to stay in this palace anymore," he replied through clenched teeth.

I stood up, still smiling. "Forgive me, my liege." I put all the sarcasm I could into my voice and curtsied mockingly. "I did not realize I was in the presence of someone with such power." I then rolled my eyes and smiled genuinely at the Wolf Lyven. Though I didn't like him, I always hated being on bad terms with anyone. I held my hand out to him. "Though I don't know why you're kind of a dirt bag, my name's Arizu. You are?"

The boy stared suspiciously at my hand, not understanding why I was being friendly all of the sudden. He tentatively took my proffered hand. "Jirsen." Jirsen let go quickly, still wearing a suspicious look. "So why were you climbing down the palace wall? It is very dangerous to do so."

I raised an eyebrow. "You do realize that I was doing fine until you caused me to fall, right? So, obviously, it's not *that* dangerous."

The Wolf Lyven pursed his lips. "Look. I'm sorry for making you fall. I didn't think before I spoke. But any further up and you would have been more than just winded after falling. You shouldn't climb without proper support anymore."

I laughed, which seemed to confuse Jirsen even more. "Thanks, Dad. I'll keep that in mind." Then, just to bother the Wolf Lyven, I turned around and began climbing the wall once more.

"Seriously?" Jirsen snapped.

I grinned, though he couldn't see my face. "Well, I was

going to take a look around the gardens, but you've ruined my sight-seeing mood. So good-bye!" I continued to climb.

"Please stop!" Jirsen sounded worried as I got higher. "I can show you the best places in the garden if you come back down! Just, please. You're freaking me out. I'm really afraid you're going to get hurt!"

"Wow. You're such a worry wort," I said teasingly. "I haven't even made it that high." To prove my point, I jumped from the wall and landed nimbly on my feet beside Jirsen. The Wolf Lyven let out a sigh of relief when he saw I was safely on the ground once again.

"What are you, some kind of climbing police?"

Jirsen looked away. "No. I just hate seeing people put themselves in danger for no reason."

I shrugged. "I honestly don't see why me doing so is any of your business. But I'm getting a free tour out of this whole situation, so lead onward!"

True to his word, the Wolf Lyven showed me the best locations in the garden. My first impression of him aside, he was actually fairly nice company. Too serious for his own good, but I could tell that he was an honest Lyven.

As we walked and talked, I found out that he and his family had been invited to the royal ball just like Roxlin's family and me had been (albeit they had to pass the examination whereas our family was invited specifically by the King and Queen). I had actually heard of Jirsen's family before, briefly, when I had overheard Viern talking about the other prominent Lyven families in the High-Class hierarchy some time before. Just as Roxlin was a part of her family's Coluber Legacy, Jirsen was part of the Hokkaido Legacy.

The sun was setting by the time I got my fill of sightseeing. Finally feeling ready to head back to my room, I told Jirsen, and he responded with one of his frequent stern looks. "You aren't going to climb back up the wall, are you?"

"It's the fastest way to get to my room!" I argued with a smirk.

Jirsen raised an eyebrow. "That's it. I'm escorting you to your room. No dangerous wall climbing for you anymore."

"Ooooo, fancy. I get a royal escort." I winked jokingly, not minding the company of the Wolf Lyven for a little bit longer.

When we got there, I really hoped that Roxlin was busy with something else so that she wouldn't feel or hear me returning since I was supposed to have been asleep or at least still in my room.

After opening my door, I turned and faced Jirsen. "Thank you. For showing me the gardens. I consider your debt for making me fall paid in full."

Jirsen smiled. I couldn't help but notice that it was a very nice-looking smile. I felt my cheeks begin to burn. "Alright see ya bye!" tumbled from my mouth and I quickly shut the door in the Wolf Lyven's face. I buried my face in my hands and mentally screamed at myself in embarrassment.

Way to go, Arizu. He probably thinks you're a super dork now. I quickly shook that thought away. *Who cares if he thinks that? I'm probably never going see him again.*

With that, I lightly smacked my red cheeks and got ready for bed. Having pushed what happened this morning from my mind, I happily climbed under the covers of my fluffy mattress afterwards.

Tired, I fell asleep thinking about what Jirsen's hair would look like if it wasn't gelled back.

I wish I hadn't fallen to sleep. I dreamed I was in a fancy hallway. Maybe a hallway of the palace? I couldn't tell. I was too terrified of the creatures chasing me.

At least three Corrupted surged after me as I ran as fast as I could to get away from them. When I turned a corner, I bumped into someone. I felt myself plead for the Lyven to help me. But she only grinned wickedly and pushed me to the ground, just as the wave of Corrupted turned the corner as well. I felt my mouth open in a scream but, just like in the other nightmares I'd had, I couldn't hear a sound. My vision fell black as the only noise I heard were the familiar words, *"Blood ties to fate. Fate is tied to blood. My blood ties me to my fate."*

I awoke to a darkened room, pinned down to my bed. I struggled as I tried to see who was holding me in place. I froze in shock at who I saw. The Eagle Lyven who I thought might be a part of Kiara's group stared down at me. His eyes peered at me with the same softness I had noticed when he had looked at me before.

"I'm sorry." He let go of my shoulders. "You were thrashing about in your sleep. It was making my job hard."

I sat up, panting from exertion, and cocked my head in question. "Are you here to protect me, too?"

The Eagle Lyven looked down in shame as he pulled a knife from a concealed sheath. "No. Quite the opposite, actually. I'm here to kill you."

Chapter 14
Roxlin

The vibrations of soft footfalls inside my room woke me. I stiffened in suspense, but tried to keep my breathing deep and regular to make it seem as if I were still asleep. My feet were facing the majority of the room, so turning my head to try and see who was walking towards my bed would be useless. I continued to lay as still as possible even as the owner of the footsteps stopped beside my bed. But I couldn't hold still any longer when I heard something metallic, and probably sharp, being drawn.

I kicked out towards the unknown intruder and caught him in the midriff. I heard a grunt of pain and felt the Lyven stumble back. Jumping out of bed, I ran for the door of my room. Whoever it was attacking me was fast, and I barely made it five steps before he caught me by the arm and threw me backwards.

I slid across the ground, but before I had traveled far, I was changed to my snake form. I heard a curse as my small, dark form slithered silently through the golden carpet. Unfortunately, in this form I couldn't even reach the doorknob of my room, let alone open the door. And I was too big to fit through the crack under the door.

Thinking fast, I made my way under my bed, trying to figure out a plan to get out of this dangerous predicament.

Whoever this Lyven was, he had obviously come to harm me, possibly even kill me. Why, I didn't know. What I did know, was that I was stuck.

"Roxlin, dear," a familiar, yet now chilling, voice said. "Please stop hiding. In that form, you can't escape me." My bed was suddenly flung onto its side, and a leopard stood above me, his muscles rippling in the violet moonlight that shone in from my balcony door.

Knowing I wasn't fast enough to escape, I lunged forward and buried my fangs into the leopard's front left leg. I cursed that I wasn't a poisonous type of snake and continued to dig my fangs in best I could as the leopard hissed in pain. He shook his foreleg vigorously and managed to fling me away.

I flew through the air and crashed straight through the glass doors of the balcony, barely managing to keep from sliding off between the supports of the railing when I landed. Glass shards cut through my scales, and I dazedly wondered why getting cut by glass seemed to be a thing for me.

The leopard bounded over to me immediately, giving me no time to gather my wits. He raised his uninjured right foreleg to give a finishing blow. But an alligator landing on his back made him crumple in surprise.

Taking the sudden distraction as an opportunity, I changed to my humanoid form and scrambled back, tensely watching as the leopard, who could only be Kren, slip out from underneath Kaylon.

Kren leaped back lithely and crouched, ready to pounce on his new opponent. Being the only vulnerable spot on Kaylon's body that he could reach, Kren swiped at Kaylon's eyes, trying to blind him. But the alligator's snapping jaws and quick turns kept the Leopard Lyven from achieving his goal.

Using my ability on Kren, I tried to figure out a way to help Kaylon. I saw with my ability that one of Kren's deepest fears was the loss of a loved one. Cursing this useless information, I began throwing chunks of glass at the leopard. Kren backed away from Kaylon and me, hissing.

Taking advantage of the respite, Kaylon said, "Kren, stop this. I know what you desire. I can see it. But allowing the Corruption to take over this world won't bring her back. Killing Roxlin doesn't even help in releasing the Corruption. So why are you targeting her?"

Kren's amber eyes flashed menacingly. "She knows too much. She found *the book*. *Sixteen years* I've been searching for that book, but someone had hidden it from me. Had hidden it from anyone who wanted to use it. However, now that Roxlin has found it, I can finally destroy it. And by killing her, no one will know its contents anymore. Not even the monarchs themselves. No one, nor anything, will be able to stop the Corruption."

"Well unfortunately for you, if you try to harm Roxlin even just one more time, I will kill you." Kren and Kaylon stared at each other, the air thick with tension. Finally, Kaylon said, "You can't bring the dead back to life. Especially not by fully releasing the Corruption. So stop living in the past. Move on. And leave this place at once." The two predators stared at each other for a few heartbeats more, and then Kren finally backed off, shifting to his humanoid form.

Standing to his full height, he towered over Kaylon, who was still in his alligator form, and me. Kren calmly walked over and picked up his knife from where he had dropped it during the struggle.

As he opened the door to leave, he turned his head and looked directly at me. "At least we managed to kill the most important pawn," he said with a malicious grin. And then he was gone. I felt my heart drop.

"What did he mean by that, Kaylon?"

Kaylon shifted back to his other form and began looking me over, worried. "You're all cut up. Here. Let me take you to Mina." The Alligator Lyven gently took my arm and tried to lead me out the door after Kren, but I jerked away from him.

Dread filled me as I took off towards Arizu's room. Kren couldn't have meant her, could he? She wasn't dead. No way. Ignoring my stinging cuts, I arrived at Arizu's door and banged as loud as I could, not caring if anyone would be bothered by me. "Arizu! Arizu, open up!" I felt Kaylon's presence next to me and I spun around to face him. "What's happened to my cousin?" I demanded, fear racing through me.

"I- I don't know. My dad went to help her, though, so I'm sure she's fi. . ."

I began banging on Arizu's door once again before he had even finished his sentence.

Finally, the door opened. Kiara peered around the frame, her small figure almost lost in the shadows. When she recognized us, she let Kaylon and me into the room.

"Where's Arizu? Is she okay?" I asked Kiara.

The Fox Lyven looked away, not meeting my gaze. "She's alive, for now. Mina was able to heal some of her wound, but any more, and Mina would have to use some of her life force. However, it may still come to that if Arizu loses anymore blood."

With that, I rushed over to Arizu's bed. Two Lyvens, Mina and who I assumed to be her and Kaylon's father, knelt on either side of the bed. I fell to my knees next to my cousin's head, a short distance from Mina.

The Dingo Lyven's face was pale, and I could see blood, so much blood, pooled around her still form. Her breath came in quick, shallow gasps, and her eyes were shut tight in pain. However, even as I watched, Arizu's face began to relax, her breathing so quiet now that I could barely hear it.

"I'm sorry, Feyor," Kiara said to the other Horse Lyven, placing a hand on his shoulder. "We *can't* lose Arizu." She turned to Mina. "Do it." Mina obediently reached under Arizu's tattered shirt and placed her hand on Arizu's stomach, the source of all the blood. No mystical glow indicated that my cousin was being healed, but her breathing deepened, and Mina. . .

Mina was aging rapidly. Being a twin to Kaylon, she was seventeen years old. But by the time she took her hand from Arizu's stomach, she now looked to be in her late twenties. This probably wouldn't seem like such a big deal to a human. Arizu had told me how fast they aged. However, Lyvens' bodies aged slower after reaching around twenty years, even though we didn't necessarily live longer than humans. We usually looked about three quarters of our actual age. So for Mina to look to be in her late twenties. . . Her actual age must be around the late thirties. More than double her original age.

With Arizu's face regaining color and her breathing stabilized, I turned to and bowed my head to Mina. I remembered her fear of violent deaths that I had seen with my ability. I felt ashamed of using that knowledge to threaten her in Ulon's Ice Cream all those days before. I now owed her a greater debt than I could ever repay. "Thank you. Thank you so much," I said. "You've sacrificed so much of your life force to keep her alive... Thank you."

Mina patted me on the head. "Even though I don't know why Arizu is so vital to our cause, I have faith in our rulers. I truly believe that we need her alive. So I'm glad to sacrifice some of my life in order to keep her breathing."

Mina's voice had gotten deeper, and her brown hair now hung far below her shoulders. And when we stood up, I noticed that she was a few inches taller as well.

"Arizu and I will forever be in your debt. If you ever need anything, just let us know. We will do anything we can to fulfill your request."

Mina place a hand on my shoulder. "Arizu fulfilling her duty will be plenty to repay your debts. It's the reason I did this anyways." A loud *thump* grabbed our attention away from our conversation. We looked over in time to see Feyor about to punch a knocked down Kaylon.

"This is your fault!" Feyor said, obviously furious. "You were on guard to protect Arizu tonight, and what did you do? Protect Roxlin instead of your charge! Because you couldn't follow a simple order, Arizu almost died. And now your sister gave up her life force to fix *your* mistake."

Kaylon's eyes burned in rage from where he sat on the ground. "If I hadn't acted as I did, Roxlin would be dead!"

"So what?" Feyor punched, and Kaylon barely managed to roll out of the way. "She's inconsequential. Do you know who isn't, though? The girl you almost let get killed. If I hadn't sensed that something was wrong, no one would have been here to stop Selen from finishing his job!" The Horse Lyven's hand flashed out and he grabbed Kaylon by the front of his shirt. "You swore an oath when you joined our group. If you can't follow through with the promise you made, *you will be dismissed.*" With that, Feyor let go of his son, turned away, and walked over to Mina. Kissing her cheek, he said, "I'm sorry, my dear daughter." With a cold look shot at me, he then promptly left the room.

Kaylon picked himself up and stood with his head bowed and his hands clenched. He then glanced at me. "I'm sorry for not protecting Arizu. But I wouldn't change my actions even if I could." Kaylon looked down again. "Sorry, Mina."

Mina smiled. "It's alright," she said. "We're all gonna die someday, and it could be at anytime. Don't worry. I've made my peace. Dad was just overreacting. This is honestly the best outcome of the situation. Everyone is alive, where-as Roxlin would be dead if it weren't for you." Kaylon still looked slightly ashamed, though not guilty. I, on the other hand, was feeling torn inside.

On one hand, Kaylon *had* saved my life, and I was grate-ful for that. But on the other hand, what if Arizu had really died because he hadn't been here to protect her? I would have never been able to forgive him.

Kiara walked over as I was grappling with my feelings

and said to me, "Selen mentioned that you have a book called *Blood Ties* in your possession?" She gestured to a shadowy form sitting with his hands tied behind his back. "He said that that's why you were also targeted." I started in shock when I noticed the shadowy figure of Selen. I hadn't even realized that anyone was sitting there. I was usually very perceptive, but I guess the panic of Arizu being hurt had captured my full attention.

"That's right," I replied. "Kren said the same thing. What I don't get is why that book is so important, though. I was reading it a bit yesterday evening, and it only seems like a journal of some sort."

"It may not seem like it, but it's actually the most important book in all of Cillium." Kiara gave a sigh. "My group and I have been waiting for it to reappear for more than a decade. We don't know exactly *why* that book is so important, but the King and Queen do." The Fox Lyven looked thoughtful for a moment, then said, "When Arizu wakes up, no matter what the monarchs say, I'm bringing you both to them. It's time we all find out what's really going on as well as how to stop the Corruption completely."

"Really?" I asked, hopeful.

Kiara nodded. "This whole secrecy thing needs to end."

I looked over at Arizu's sleeping form. Smiling, I said quietly, "You hear that, Arizu? We're finally gonna learn what's going on! So just hang on for a little longer." I then glanced at Selen, tipping my head in question. "How did you get him to talk so easily, anyways?"

Kiara chuckled. "I'm a biochemical engineer. I know what substances to mix to make an elixir that loosens the tongue."

"Sweet," I said, impressed. Kiara smiled slightly and then signaled Kaylon over to her. I still didn't know what to feel about his actions, so I quickly turned back to Mina.

While Kaylon and Kiara talked, Mina healed my cuts, and then I left to change into different, non-bloody, non-ripped, pajamas. After changing, I grabbed some blankets and a pillow and headed back over to Arizu's room. I didn't want to leave her alone after what had just happened. Especially because Kren was still free and roaming around the palace. Plus, my bed was kind of broken at the moment.

Kaylon dragged a loopy Selen out of my cousin's bedroom door as I arrived, Mina and Kiara following along behind.

"Ah, Roxlin." I looked at Kiara as she spoke. "Would you mind giving me *Blood Ties* for safe keeping?"

Suspicion immediately flared inside me. "Actually, and meaning no disrespect, I'm going to keep it with me."

"It's more dangerous that way, though. You'll still be a target if you continue to keep it."

"If Arizu is forced to be a target, I'll be a target as well." Thinking fast, I came up with the best excuse for doing so that I could muster. "This way, it splits the enemy's attention. For instance, what if Selen and Kren had come to kill Arizu at the same time?"

Kiara hesitated, then said, "It. . . Could have been a different outcome."

"Exactly."

The Fox Lyven sighed. "Fine. We'll have three guards on you both at all times from now on. Don't leave Arizu alone, and don't wander off by yourself. Doing so would end up splitting *our* attention."

"Understood." The three Lyvens then headed off, Kaylon mumbling a good-bye as he pushed Selen along.

After I dropped my bedding down next to Arizu's bed, I quickly ran back to my room and grabbed *Blood Ties* from where I had hidden it in a cupboard in my bathroom. Running back over to my cousin's room, I locked her door behind me and then made myself a make-shift bed on the floor.

Once I finished checking Arizu over one more time, I placed *Blood Ties* under my pillow, and slept the rest of the night on edge.

Chapter 15
Arizu

I was in the dark room with that single source of blue/ white light once again. The Gate shone so bright that it hurt my eyes. The only differences between being in the room this time and the time before was that I was alone, and, that I wasn't terrified of the Gate.

In this dream, instead of being tossed into the Gate, I stepped forward in confidence and placed myself into the light as my lips moved in a silent chant. Though I still couldn't hear anything, I knew from the movement of my mouth that I was saying, *"Blood ties to fate. Fate is tied to blood. My blood ties me to my fate."* The pain I had felt before seared against my flesh for a moment, and then it was gone.

. .

My eyes blinked open to sunshine. I felt refreshed. This was the first sleep I had gotten since coming to the palace that hadn't been plagued by a nightmare. It felt as though today was going to be a good day! Hopefully.

I sat up as I suddenly smelled a metallic scent. Confused, I glanced at where the smell was originating from, and was shocked to see my bed sheets as well as my pajama shirt completely covered in dry blood.

"What the. . ." I fell from my bed in surprise, landing hard atop *something*. Or, as a muttered curse made it so clear, *someone*.

"Mind getting off me, ya heifer?" Roxlin groaned from underneath me.

"Oh my gosh I'm so sorry!" I quickly rolled off of my cousin, standing up while hoping that I didn't bruise or break any parts of her. "Are you alright?"

"Besides being crushed below a whale, I'm fine." Roxlin drowsily stood up beside me. She yawned as I stared in confusion.

"Rox, what are you doing in my room? And why is there blood all over me?"

"You were stabbed," Roxlin replied simply.

"*WHAT?!*"

Even as Roxlin started to explain what had happened the previous night, I began to remember my encounter with the Eagle Lyven.

Selen, (I had learned his name from Roxlin), hadn't seemed like he wanted to hurt me. Sure, he had been prickly, especially to Aunt Viern. But it was almost as if someone had forced him to try to kill me. Ignoring that idea, however, I was excited to hear that Kiara would be getting Roxlin and me an audience with King Rolm and Queen Aulia. It was about time!

"Do you really think she can get us an audience with them?" I asked my cousin.

"I don't know for sure, but Kiara seemed confident that she could."

I shook my head. "I still can't believe that there are people who actually *want* the Corruption around. And what did Kaylon mean about releasing the Corruption fully? Is a main source of it locked away somewhere? Because it already seems to be roaming about pretty freely."

Roxlin shrugged. "Those are questions we need to save for the King and Queen."

"I guess then all we can do for now is wait?"

Roxlin shrugged again. I sighed and laid back down on my bed.

Now all I could think about at the moment was how much Mina had sacrificed to keep me alive. I felt so guilty for being a burden yet again, only this time it had ended with a steep price.

It also didn't help that this strange *"force"* inside of me kept pushing me to hurt people. When Selen had raised his knife to kill me, I had felt that same darkness attacking me from within as I had when I'd almost killed Avo and when Roxlin and I had been in the library. Trying to fight the dark desire back had distracted me to the point that I hadn't even tried to defend myself against Selen. He had stabbed me in the stomach as easily as if I had been a defenseless babe.

But the dark force inside of me scared me more than dying.

I scared me more than anything.

"Get up, Ari." Roxlin's voice shook me from my stupor. "No sense in letting our time waste away like this. If Sou isn't coming this morning, we should go find ourselves something to eat."

I nodded. "Let's get ready, first. I want to wash this blood off me." I quickly hopped out of bed, got some clean clothes, and then went to the bathroom to take a shower.

Upon returning to the main room, I found Roxlin dressed up in one of her best dresses.

It was a dark blue formal-looking dress. A black sash wrapped around her waist and came together in a bow at the back, tying the outfit together.

I had to admit. I was kind of jealous of how good she looked. Having never really worn dresses in my entire life, I usually felt awkward in them.

Guessing from the way she was dressed that Kiara had managed to pull off convincing the King and Queen to have a meeting with us, I asked Roxlin if such was true.

"Yep. Sou informed me of it while you were still in the shower. She said to be ready for when Kiara comes to take us to them. But first. . ."

Roxlin gestured to two trays on my desk. "Sou also brought us some breakfast. And after we finish eating, she told me to give you something."

"Ooo what is it?"

"You'll know soon enough. Now let's eat."

Once finished with our meal, Roxlin reached under the desk and pulled a pretty yellow spring dress from out of a paper bag.

"Woah where did Sou get that dress?" I lightly touched the fine fabric of the dress. "It's so pretty!"

"I don't know. But she knows that you don't really have any actual formal wear here on Cillium, and that you probably wouldn't want to meet the King and Queen in a T-shirt and pants. So she got you something nice to wear."

I bounced up and down in excitement. "Oh my gosh this is awesome! Is it really mine?" Roxlin raised an eyebrow. "You're right," I laughed. "Stupid question." I took the dress from Roxlin and held it up to me. "I can't wait to try it on!"

I quickly skipped to the bathroom to get changed. To my delight, the dress fit perfectly. And when I emerged, I twirled around my room to show the dress off. "I can't get over how pretty it is! I definitely need to thank Sou when I see her next." I was too happy to even feel uncomfortable in the dress.

Roxlin gave a slight smile. "That's a good idea. She also brought you some shoes. Here." My cousin threw a pair of white flats at my feet.

I had just slipped the flats on when a knock came at my door. I ran and opened it.

"Ready to meet the King and Queen of Cillium?" Kiara asked with a triumphant smile.

"You betcha!" I replied enthusiastically.

Roxlin came and stood beside me. "It's about time, too. I thought Arizu and I would be dead by the time they kicked things into gear."

Kiara sighed as she began leading us onward to the audience chamber. "That wouldn't really have surprised me, honestly. It actually seemed like they were going to refuse my request at first, but they gave in immediately when I mentioned that you had found *Blood Ties*."

"What is *with* that book?" Roxlin asked, exasperated. "I've been reading it, and though I haven't made it that far yet, it really doesn't seem like it can help your cause of getting rid of the Corruption. Whoever wrote it seems to be trying to stay away from the Corruption more than trying to get rid of it."

"I don't know," Kiara responded. "That's why we're meeting with the King and Queen."

Despite my anxiety, nervousness, and excitement of finally being able to meet with the monarchs of Cillium, I couldn't help but still marvel at the beauty of the palace. The amazing architecture and decor still made me stare in awe. And then we made it to the doors of the audience chamber.

Much like how palace doors are depicted in fictional books, these were huge white and black oak doors, as thick as I was wide. They were at least twelve feet tall, as well. Expertly carved imagery in the oak depicted scenes of Cillium's history, much like the stain glass dome at the entrance of the palace.

Pausing before the grand doors, Kiara turned to my cousin and me. "Are you girls ready?" In unison, Roxlin and I nodded. Despite her small stature, Kiara seemed to push the huge doors open with ease. We entered.

The audience chamber wasn't as large or as finely decorated as I had expected it to be, but it was still as imposing as the rest of the palace. Massive pillars lined the room from the entrance to a raised dais at the far end of the room. No rugs decorated the floor, and where art usually hung along the walls, large and very old tapestries took their place. Where artificial lights lit up the rest of the palace, thousands of candles provided the only illumination here. It was like all modernization had been kept from being implemented here.

At the far end of the audience chamber, resting atop the

dais, were two large thrones that looked to be made from the same type of oak as the entrance doors. And sitting upon those, were the King and Queen of Cillium.

"Welcome," King Rolm's voice boomed. "Please, come forward, Kiara the Fox, Roxlin the Snake, and Arizu the Dingo. My wife and I have much anticipated our long-awaited chat."

"Well you sure didn't show it with how long you took," Roxlin mumbled under her breath. I shot her a "are you mad?!" kind of look, but my cousin just shrugged, unapologetic.

As the three of us stopped in front of the thrones, I noticed that there were no guards anywhere to be seen. Were the monarchs just not worried about their safety? Or were the topics we were going to be discussing so secret that not even trusted guards were allowed to hear?

Now being able to see the King and Queen up close, they were exactly as how I imagined royalty to look. King Rolm was clean shaven, had short cropped black hair, and wore a fitted suit. His eyes were so dark that it seemed almost as if he had no pupils. With a strong jaw and thick eyebrows, he would have looked stern and unapproachable if he hadn't been smiling, which softened his features exponentially.

Queen Aulia looked quite the opposite of her husband. She had rounded cheeks and large gray eyes that gave her an innocent look. Curly, reddish-brown hair fell just below her shoulders, and she stood regally beside the King in a red, form fitting gown as her husband rose to greet us. And, interestingly, it was impossible to tell what Lyven either royal had been before becoming the King and Queen.

Further examination found that they both looked to

be in their mid-forties, which would mean their actual age would be somewhere around sixty.

Roxlin had mentioned when we were discussing the topic of Cillium's King and Queen, once, that they would probably be naming an heir to the throne soon since they were getting up there in age. Though, I had never heard of King Rolm and Queen Aulia having a child, so I didn't know how that would all work. Growing up mostly on Earth, I didn't know a lot about how Cillium's leadership worked.

Kiara, Roxlin, and I all bowed in respect to the rulers of this world.

King Rolm waved us up. "Thank you for coming. Though this room is fine for less important meetings, we will be using a safer location than here. Follow us, please." Turning, the monarchs led the way to the wall behind the thrones, and, after a strange set of symbols had been revealed and pressed in a specific pattern, a secret door that had blended in seamlessly with the rest of the wall opened without a sound.

The Queen ushered the three of us through the door and into what would be considered a modest sized room. Especially when compared to the rest of the rooms of the palace that I had seen.

The door was shut tightly behind the five of us. Kiara must have been here before, for she didn't seem surprised at suddenly being told to enter into a strange, secret room. I, on the other hand, took everything in with wide eyes. Not that there was much to see in this new place.

No furniture or decorations were in this room save it be eight chairs placed in a circle facing each other with a simple round table in the center of them. The set up reminded me of

King Arthur's round table. Though the Lyvens' wouldn't know what that story was if I made a reference to it. Again, candles placed in holders along the walls were the only light source.

"Take a seat, and we'll begin" the King told us.

Unlike the uncomfortable looking oak thrones outside, these chairs had padding on them and seemed comfy to sit on. So I quickly settled down onto one and made myself comfortable, anticipation flowing through me. Kiara and Roxlin took a seat on either side of me, and the monarchs sat across from us.

"Thank you for being patient with us," Queen Aulia said. "We were planning to wait to have this meeting when one of you two found *Blood Ties*," she gestured to Roxlin and me, "and we didn't expect it to reveal itself on only your first full day here at the palace."

"It's definitely been frustrating," I said, dipping my head in respect. "But we understand that you must have your reasons."

King Rolm nodded, his smile gone and a serious look now taking its place. "Yes, we did. And with that, let's get down to business. I'm sure your first questions will be about the Corruption, so let's start there. This will be a history lesson of sorts, so continue to bear with us." The King cleared his throat, and then began his explanation.

"A *very* long time ago, Lyvens used to live on Earth." I accidentally cut King Rolm off with a gasp of shock. I felt everyone's eyes upon me and flushed in embarrassment.

"Sorry," I said. Thankfully, no one commented on my outburst, and the King continued as though nothing had interrupted him.

"However, when a great evil began to overtake Earth, a hero arose to fight back the thing called the Corruption and its minions, deemed the Corrupted. But she soon found that she couldn't completely destroy the Corruption. So instead of trying to accomplish the impossible, she created a prison for it to be sealed away inside. A prison called Cillium. This is actually why Earth and Cillium are able to be connected by a Gate when no other world is.

"Knowing that guardians would be needed to keep the Corruption from ever escaping and, being a scarce bunch – for many wizards, mages, and sorcerers hunted us for the magical properties that reside in our DNA – the few remaining Lyvens at the time volunteered to be so. It was the best choice, because they knew that if they stayed on Earth, they would be hunted to extinction. Ever since then, Lyvens have lived here on Cillium, now unaware of what our duty is."

All inhabitants in the room were quiet for a moment.

"So how do you know about all of this if this seemingly *very important piece of our history* has been lost?" Roxlin asked skeptically.

Queen Aulia answered this time. "We don't know when these times were, but the Corruption has almost escaped before on several occasions, just like now. Because Lyvens had thought that the Corruption wouldn't ever be able to escape, a world-wide panic spread when Corrupted began reappearing for the first time. So the monarchs of that time decided that this knowledge should only be held by the King and Queen. Therefore, after they sealed the Corruption away once again, they erased the minds of our people, and altered the information so that it would only be passed to the next in succession at the time of their coronation. Just like how it is concerning the powers held by the King and Queen."

We were all silent again as Kiara, Roxlin, and I tried to process everything we had just heard. I was mostly silent out of mere shock, my brain seemingly frozen. If I had thought the bits and pieces of crazy information that Roxlin and I had been given and/or put together had been hard to swallow, I was, at this point, drowning in this river of new information. I felt it hard to breathe.

"So, why am I important in all of this?" I asked in a quiet voice.

King Rolm looked at me warmly, reminding me for a moment of Sou. "You, my dear girl, are the only one that can seal the Corruption away once again."

Chapter 16
Roxlin

"You, my dear girl, are the only one who can seal the Corruption away once again." I saw Arizu shrink into herself and she looked as though she was on the brink of another breakdown.

"Now hold on just a minute." I tried to keep my irritation in check. "You can't just dump something this extreme onto a sixteen-year-old girl. Arizu isn't even a full-blooded Lyven. Why should she have to deal with any of this?"

The King and Queen shared a look, and then Queen Aulia said, "Arizu. . . Doesn't actually have any human blood at all."

I heard my cousin begin to hyperventilate as she tugged on her fuzzy dingo ears. She brought her knees up to her chest and buried her face into her legs.

Panic shot through me at her condition. Just like when we had been in the library, I began rubbing her back, trying to soothe her. "Deep breaths," I said quietly. In all honesty, though, I was more scared of what Arizu would do other than just her condition at the moment. When we had been in the library, I had heard her voice. It was hers, but, somehow *different*. It was like a darker, suppressed side of Arizu had taken hold of her for a moment. It had sounded like she was about to snap. And though I was ashamed to admit it, fear pulsed through me because of that hidden side of her.

After a moment, Arizu got control of herself and shook my hand off. "Stop it," she said. I was surprised at the sudden coldness in her voice. It wasn't exactly the same as what I had heard before, but I could tell that Arizu was definitely not back to normal.

My cousin straightened in her seat, her eyes glassy. Folding her hands into her lap, she stared calmly, *too* calmly, at the King and Queen. "Explain," she demanded with that same coldness. The monarchs stiffened at her lack of respect, but they probably didn't want to upset Arizu any more, so they merely answered her question.

"Your father, Ruvon. He's a Lyven. Aulia's and my son, to be precise," King Rolm said. I waited stiffly for Arizu to break down at this revelation, but her posture remained poised and her face showed no surprise. And that's when what King Rolm had just said finally kicked my brain into gear.

"Wait *what?!* I asked incredulously. "No way. That's not possible. Arizu's dad lives on Earth. He would be dead if he were a Lyven."

King Rolm looked at me. "Like how Jaspes and Paryle are dead?" he said in response. I averted my gaze, my brain barely grasping this news. King Rolm turned back to Arizu.

"You see, the aforementioned hero foresaw that her prison wouldn't be perfect. So she created a fail- safe for if the

Corruption began to break free. This fail-safe was created by tying her spirit to her bloodline. So, whenever she was needed, she would be recalled to Cillium; reborn into a new body that carried her same ancestral heritage. A body capable of using the magic needed to once again complete the prison. She left behind a prophecy to help us know which child was her reborn.

"Figuring out that the prophecy concerned you, it made Ruvon and his wife, Zea, try to flee to Earth to avoid it. They didn't want you to have to carry this burden. So after using Paryle's ability to create the Gate found in your uncle's home and going through, she and Ruvon gave up their Lyven abilities to be able to survive on Earth. Aulia and I, of course, had to go after them. Cillium needed you, and because of your parents' foolishness in trying to hide you away, they only made things harder for everyone.

"When we found Ruvon and Zea, they wouldn't listen to reason. They tried to fight against us and, unfortunately, Zea lost her life during the struggle. Broken by her death, Ruvon agreed to let you return to Cillium with us. But on one condition.

"Because he could no longer live on Cillium due to having already abandoned his heritage as a Lyven, he requested that we allow you to live with him on Earth, and to leave you be until the day the prophecy needed to be fulfilled. In order for you to be able to survive on Earth, we had to seal most of your Lyven side away, but leave enough so that you could still pass through the Gate to Cillium. That's why you don't have an ability of your own, and why you have trouble shifting to your other form."

Arizu was staring at the far wall now. She spoke slowly. "Everything. . . makes sense now." She looked at the King, her cold demeanor melting. "Yes. Thank you for telling me this. Nothing more needs to be said. Many memories of my past lives are returning now, and I know what I need to do."

I bristled. "Hold on, Ari." I glared at the monarchs, now addressing them. "You mean to tell us that if you had just told Arizu who her father was, she could have avoided being shunned by almost every Lyven she met? Don't you think she deserves an explanation for that as well?" The King and Queen glanced at each other again.

"Arizu was being shunned?" Queen Aulia asked, clearly taken aback. "The only reason we led Arizu to believe that she was half human was so that she would feel more at home on Earth. We had no idea Arizu was being treated negatively by our people." I opened my mouth to tell the Queen how stupid that sounded, but my cousin turned to me and cut me off.

"Leave it be, Roxlin. That doesn't matter anymore." She readied herself as if to stand. "You left *Blood Ties* back in my room?" I nodded, dumbfounded. How was Arizu being so calm? She had been freaking out just a minute ago. Though, she did say that memories of her past were returning. But she shouldn't have become a completely different Lyven just because she had regained those memories. . . right?

Clenching my jaw, I turned away from her.

"Good. Let's go get it now. I need it to complete the spell that will restrain the Corruption."

"So that's why *Blood Ties* is important?" I asked Arizu, still not looking at her.

"Yes. Though a lot of my memories have returned, the words of the spell aren't among them. And *Blood Ties* carries that spell."

Queen Aulia nodded. "That's why we had been searching for the book for so long. You see, before she left, Zea used her ability to hide the book. We didn't know what the key to finding it was, but based on what happened, we can suppose that it would only reveal itself to someone that shared her blood. That must be why you, Roxlin, were able to find it. We had given up hope of it ever being found, and decided it best to bring Arizu here to see if she could at least somehow figure out what the spell was. Thankfully, we no longer have to worry about that.

"Along those same lines, we created this ball as a cover to get you, Arizu, safely here. We didn't want to alert the Corruption as to who you were by suddenly allowing a seemingly random Lyven to come stay at the palace. Though, our insistence of your presence must have tipped it off." I nodded thoughtfully. Like Arizu had said, everything was making sense now.

Kiara now spoke for the first time. "This has been very. . . Enlightening. I'm glad we all know the truth now. If no one has any more questions, I think it best to quickly get the Corruption taken care of. Anything else?" Kiara glanced at the rest of us in the room.

I was about to shake my head no, but suddenly remembered something. "Your Majesties, why is it that Kren and Selen attacked Arizu and me? How do they know about the Corruption?"

"Good question," King Rolm acknowledged. "The

Corruption," he continued, "can control its Corrupted tele-pathically. That's why you don't see them mindlessly wander-ing about causing damage. In the same way, the Corruption can reach out to the minds of some Lyvens. From what we've gathered, it promises the Lyvens something they desperately desire. Kaylon has been instrumental in figuring this out."

"But, why doesn't it just attack us using the Corrupted?"

"It's actually thanks to Kiara that they haven't been a big problem this time around," Arizu said. I turned to my cousin, surprised that she knew the reason. "In the past," she continued, "we didn't have her skill in biochemical engineer-ing. She's been able to keep their numbers to a minimum by finding the non-hosted Corruption and taking care of it, and by inventing the vaccine that allows her, Kaylon, Mina, and Feyor to touch and destroy them." Arizu looked up at the ceiling. "Perhaps, with this advancement," she said in a soft voice, "the Corruption may someday be fully destroyed." She gave a rueful smile. "I can't believe I forgot my past until now. Looks like my life wasn't worthless after all. . ."

I couldn't bring myself to say anything to that, and after a moment of silence, Arizu shook herself. "Enough distrac-tions. It's time to finish this." She stood, and the rest of us followed suit.

Back in the audience chamber, Kiara, Arizu, and I bowed to the monarchs, then took our leave. We headed straight to Arizu's room.

Anticipation made me jumpy. I didn't know why, but I had a bad feeling about something. And it wasn't helping that Kiara and Arizu didn't speak a single word on the way.

Normally I would have been fine with the silence. But

being quiet wasn't Arizu. At least, not the Arizu I knew. Usually, she'd have been talking nonstop over what we had just learned Or, if distressed about the news, she'd have been trying to keep her mind off it by talking about something else. This sudden silence of hers was almost unbearable.

We opened the door to my cousin's room. The balcony doors stood open wide. And standing over Arizu's bed was a familiar figure. In her hands was *Blood Ties*.

"*Mother?*" I asked, my surprise almost instantaneously turning to anger. Kiara acted immediately, sprinting towards the Snake Lyven. But before she could reach my mother, the Snake grinned maliciously, stepped back into the shadows of the room, and disappeared from view. Kiara cursed.

"She's still in here!" I called. "Arizu, block the door! Kiara, the balcony!" I rushed towards the balcony door, in sync with Kiara. But once again, we were too late.

My mother flickered back into view on the balcony, now in snake form. The book laid beside her. And, to my frustration, a large eagle swooped down, picked up the book in one talon and my mother in the other, and flew off.

"*No!*" Kiara tried to jump from the balcony railing to try to retake the book, but I quickly grabbed her arm and yanked her back. The fall wouldn't have necessarily killed her, but it wouldn't have ended pleasantly.

Kiara puffed angrily beside me. "I should have killed him. I *knew* locking him up wouldn't be enough."

I gave the Fox Lyven a questioning stare. "Kren? Was that who the eagle was? How did he get out of prison?"

Kiara glared at where Kren and my mother had disappeared from view. "I'm assuming Viern had a hand in his escape. That ability of hers is ridiculous." The Fox Lyven growled. "Now we have to track them down before they have the opportunity to destroy *Blood Ties*." Bitterness coated her voice. "Though, finding them is going to be impossible."

I glanced at Arizu, wondering why she still hadn't said a word. My cousin stood near the door still, staring thoughtfully at the ground. Her posture, the expression she was making, it was all so different from the Arizu I had known my whole life. It made me feel uneasy.

Suddenly, Arizu clapped her hands together. "This is an unexpected delay," she said. "But fortunately, I believe my memories will fully return to me at any moment. It's inconvenient to have to visit the King and Queen again so soon, but we should inform them of this circumstance."

Unexpected delay? Inconvenient? Inform them of this circumstance? This wasn't how Arizu talked. It was all wrong. However, I swallowed my discomfort and kept silent on the trip back to King Rolm and Queen Aulia, only speaking when spoken to.

After the debriefing, Arizu made one last statement before we left. She bowed in respect to our monarchs. "King Rolm, Queen Aulia. I apologize for maybe speaking out of place. However, if possible, I believe we should move the ball to be in two days time."

The King and Queen looked confused.

"And why would that be?" Queen Aulia asked.

"I believe the memory of the spell will come back very soon, and I. . . Was actually looking forward to the ball. All the Lyvens invited are here already, correct?" Arizu smiled, and I was able to glimpse the old version of my cousin for a moment. I felt relief at knowing that the Arizu I knew was still in there, even if she seemed mostly buried at the moment.

The Queen smiled back. "Yes, that can be arranged." She clasped her hands together. "The royal ball will be held in two days time!"

Chapter 17
Arizu

It was the morning of the ball. Though the days leading up to the big night had been hectic with preparations, no more attacks from the Corruption came. It was nice to have a breather. Which was probably on no small part contributed by the high security Kiara had placed around Roxlin and me. The extra Lyvens constantly around us were a nuisance, sure. But some time spent worrying about nothing except making sure our gowns fit was worth it.

"These are beautiful," I told the seamstresses that afternoon. Roxlin and I had just stopped at where the women worked to pick up our newly finished dresses for the ball. And to our delight, they had been beautifully created.

Roxlin's gown was dark emerald with small white gemstones placed haphazardly over the bodice and skirt. A white lace band around the waist led down to a split in the front that revealed the sleek white fabric of the underskirt. Long white gloves and white high-heels were the finishing touches.

Mine was more of a ballgown style, but just as elegant as my cousin's. It was teal with black embroidery along the skirt that reached up about a fourth of the way. A thin, black, see-through mesh flowed over the skirt from the waist down. The bodice was simple, but a black sash wound around the waist and my favorite flower, a Crystal Rose, sat to the right and on top of the sash. Three black diamonds, two smaller ones on either side of a slightly bigger one, followed the curve of the neckline. Long black gloves and sparkly black flats completed my outfit.

"It was our pleasure to design these for you," the seamstresses said in unison and with a bow. Bowing in return and leaving with a final thank-you, Roxlin and I headed back to our rooms to finish our preparations for the night. Our guards followed a respectful distance behind.

On the way, Roxlin fidgeted with her dress, seeming as though she wanted to ask me something.

"Is something bothering you?" I prompted her.

Roxlin kept her gaze on her dress. "I've been meaning to ask you about your. . . *episodes*," she said hesitantly.

I chuckled. "You mean when I would go all psycho for a little bit?" Roxlin nodded, still keeping her eyes elsewhere.

I faced forward as we walked onward, now serious. "Do you remember what King Rolm said about how the Corruption communicates with Lyvens?" Roxlin nodded again. I continued, "In the same way, the Corruption was attacking my mind when it felt I was at my weakest. It was pushing my negative emotions, trying to break me. But you don't have to worry about that anymore. I've remembered how keep it out of my head."

"I see. That's good to hear." We walked the rest of the way to our rooms in silence.

I attempted to relax before the ball, but it was useless. And before I knew it, the time had finally arrived for Roxlin and I to journey to the ballroom.

Standing together outside our rooms, Sou and Kiara stood next to us, having helped us with makeup and hair. Thankfully, Kiara had ordered the Lyvens assigned to guard us to watch from a distance tonight so we'd be able to enjoy ourselves to the fullest extent.

Sou was sniffling, tears having welled up in her eyes as she looked at Roxlin and me. "You girls look so grown up and so, so beautiful." She enveloped us both in a gentle hug. "I'm so thankful to have been given the opportunity to live by your sides. I know it was a shock to learn that I was placed into the Coluber household by King Rolm and Queen Aulia to keep an eye on Arizu. But just know. Watching you two grow up has been the most wonderful thing that has happened to me."

I smiled warmly at the Bear Lyven as she pulled away from Roxlin and me. The old me would have probably started crying at Sou's heart-warming words, but the memories from my previous lives had hardened my soul. I had seen too much and had been betrayed too often to cry just because of a few fluffy words.

"She's right." Kiara gave us an approving nod of her head. "You both look stunning. Probably going to be the stars of the night."

Roxlin scoffed. "Great. Like we needed any more attention drawn to us." Responses between agreeing with Roxlin or telling her to not worry so much fought to leave my mouth. In the end, I forced myself to be silent. The thoughts from the Lyven I had grown up to be and the thoughts formed from previous experiences didn't seem to be mixing well. Though, that wouldn't matter, soon.

"Let's go," I said, letting Kiara take the lead as she guided us through the palace to where the ballroom was located. When we reached the entrance, Sou and Kiara left us.

I had seen the ballroom before in my third and fourth lives, and not much had changed. It was still a wide, open, spectacular golden room with three brilliant, glowing chandeliers hanging from a high ceiling. Polished to a shine, the dark, onyx marble flooring was covered by guests, waiters, and waitresses. Tables sat around the perimeter of the dance floor, and fancy food tables on either side of the room held a variety of Cillium delicacies. Finally, musicians at the far end of the magnificent room were playing welcoming music atop a grand stage.

Only minor differences stood out from what I remembered – the art and tapestries that adorned the walls had changed over the years.

"Now announcing Lady Roxlin of the Coluber Legacy, and Lady Arizu!" An announcer to the right of the entry called out. Though a few heads turned toward at us newcomers, we were mostly ignored. Which suited me just fine.

I nodded to the announcer and continued walking, excited to see the new dances my people would have come up with while my spirit had been away. Dancing had always been one of my favorite hobbies.

Following closely beside me, Roxlin said, "I hadn't realized so many Lyvens had been invited. It seems as though even some important families in the Middle-Class are here."

"Yes. The King and Queen had a good idea when they decided to use this as a cover to get me into the palace. Too bad it didn't exactly work out," I replied.

"I think that's an understatement," Roxlin said dryly. She then nodded towards the area closest to the musicians. The King and Queen mingled there with their subjects, in plain view. "Speaking of the King and Queen, there they are. Should we go say hi?"

I shook my head. "No. I have nothing of importance to report to them, and if they need us, they'll search us out."

Roxlin nodded. "Makes sense."

Staying to the outskirts of the throng, Roxlin and I watched the many couples on the dance floor twirl together to an upbeat orchestral piece. However, it wasn't long before our peaceful vigil was interrupted by two well-dressed boys. They looked a little older than us, and carried a haughty air about them.

"Hello, ladies," the taller one on the right said.

"We couldn't help but notice how lonely you both looked," the blonde one on the left continued.

"Mind if we accompany you tonight?" the taller one finished.

"Trust me, we'd rather be lonely than have your company," Roxlin said scathingly. "A pair of rocks are more appealing."

The Lyvens' expressions soured. "A simple no would have sufficed," the blonde one said with an indignant huff.

"Would you have listened if we had merely stated no?" I asked him in an even tone. Both boys opened their mouths to say something, but before they could, a familiar voice cut in.

"I'm sure these lovely ladies would have had a splendid time with such nice gentlemen as yourselves. . ." Roxlin scoffed at that, "but I'm afraid we already have that honor."

We? I wondered. I knew immediately that the voice belonged to Kaylon. He slipped easily beside Roxlin, but a presence to my left caught me off guard. I turned my head and was surprised to see the serious-faced Jirsen standing there.

Both wore black suits, the only difference being the ties. Kaylon wore a white tie, and Jirsen wore a red one.

A sharp stab of nervousness shot through my stomach at seeing the Wolf Lyven, but I quickly shoved the silly feeling down. There was no time for crushes.

Though they looked miffed at the situation, the two unknown boys backed away and left the four of us alone.

I bowed my head to Kaylon and Jirsen and said, "Thank you. It would have probably taken a while to get those two to leave if you guys hadn't come."

"It was no problem," Kaylon replied. "You see, I couldn't let some random Lyven come steal Roxlin away from me." He grinned in Roxlin's direction as she rolled her eyes and quickly turned away.

"Men our age can get dangerously aggressive when told no. It could have turned into a very bad situation." Jirsen gave me a look as he said this. "It seems as though someone likes danger, however."

I shrugged and gave a slight grin at Jirsen's jab.

"Uh, who are you?" Roxlin asked the Wolf Lyven.

Jirsen turned to her. "My name is Jirsen, of the Hokkaido Legacy."

"Ah, yes. I know your family. Quite a stiff lot you are."

"We are merely cautious. That is all."

Kaylon cleared his throat and tapped my cousin on the shoulder, grabbing her attention from her skepticism. "Will you allow me the pleasure of a dance?"

Roxlin hesitated, but as she started raising her hand to accept, the music ended. She quickly snatched her hand back, and I saw annoyance flash across Kaylon's face as he glanced at the musicians.

When Kaylon turned back to my cousin, he wore his easy grin once again. "Perhaps the next dance?"

Roxlin looked away. "Maybe." I gave a small smile at what was happening in front of me. Same old Roxlin. *I* may have changed, but it was reassuring to know that my cousin hadn't changed even after all the stuff we had been through.

"That sounds like a good idea," Jirsen said, facing straight and not meeting my eyes.

"What? A dance?" I wondered with a smirk. "Are you sure that's not too dangerous for you?" Jirsen shot me an exasperated look. I chuckled. "Alright, alright. I'd love to dance with you." I looked over to see if Roxlin had agreed to dance with Kaylon, and saw that she had disappeared. "Where did Roxlin go?" I asked a slightly dejected looking Kaylon.

"She said she'd be back when the next song started, but I'm not sure she's gonna come back."

I placed a hand on Kaylon's shoulder. "Don't worry. I'm here, so she'll be back."

True to my words, as soon as the next song began to play – a slow song this time – Roxlin was back. Only not alone.

Beside her walked a Spider Lyven. She had four dark

eyes and long brown hair. Wearing a silver gown, she was quite pretty.

Kaylon's face paled as the girls approached. "Who's your friend there, Roxlin?" He clenched his teeth but forced a smile, though it looked more like a grimace.

"This is Polj. I've met her and her family before. They're wonderful Lyvens. I was just telling Polj how I heard you say she looked very pretty tonight. So I brought her over here so that you could dance with her!" Roxlin gave Kaylon an evil grin.

Kaylon's fake smile seemed frozen in place. "That was the *kindest* thing you've *ever* done, *dear Roxlin*." The stress Kaylon placed on his words made it obvious how much he didn't want to be in this situation. Polj, thankfully, didn't seem to notice his implementation. Or at least, her shy expression didn't change.

Kaylon bowed to the Spider Lyven. "Forgive me for my seeming discomfort. I'm just so nervous at the presence of one so beautiful."

Polj blushed and said in a quiet voice, "It's alright." With that, Kaylon stiffly reached out and took Polj's hand, pulling her in to dance.

"I'm guessing he's afraid of spiders?" I asked Roxlin with a raised eyebrow.

"Ooooooh yeah. Like, deathly afraid of them."

"You're a terrible Lyven."

Roxlin, still grinning evilly, just shrugged.

Jirsen cleared his throat behind me.

I turned around and faced him. "Don't worry. I haven't forgotten about you," I told him teasingly. With that, we began to dance.

Despite what I had thought earlier, and despite the memories of my pasts, the me right now was still only sixteen years old. And Jirsen was reeeeeaaaaally good-looking. I felt my stomach tie in knots as we danced. We didn't talk much, but it wasn't because of awkwardness. It was more like we just, didn't need to talk.

When the song finished, Roxlin, Kaylon, Jirsen, and I met up once again.

"Where's Polj?" Roxlin asked Kaylon as soon as she saw him.

"The lovely lady said she needed to use the bathroom," he replied with a glare.

"Well, that's just unfortunate. I was hoping to talk to her some more."

Still glaring at the innocent-looking Roxlin, Kaylon said, "Yes. . . Very unfortunate. . ."

"Are you thirsty, Arizu?" Jirsen asked me. "I can get you something to drink, if you want."

"Water sounds great. Thank you, Jirsen."

The Wolf Lyven nodded and headed off to the nearest food table.

"Despite what you did to me, I'm still a gentleman. So, *dear Roxlin*, would you like something to drink as well?" Kaylon asked my cousin.

She pursed her lips. "Sure. I'll take some water too." While the boys were gone, Roxlin and I chatted about the ball. The music had started to play again, and it was fun seeing all the couples dancing in synchronization to the jaunty tune.

There *was* actually one more serious topic that I wanted

to discuss with my cousin while the boys were away, so I took this time to bring it up. "It doesn't seem to bother you that neither of your parents are here?" I stated questioningly.

Roxlin shrugged, still watching the dancing Lyvens. "My mom is nowhere to be found, and when I asked Sou about my father, all she said was that he was too ashamed at Mother's betrayal to show his face." Roxlin didn't continue, so I left the discussion there.

When the boys returned, Jirsen handed me my water, and Kaylon did the same for Roxlin. I raised the cup to my lips to take a sip, but before I could drink, Roxlin spat her water back into her cup.

"This water tastes disgusting!" she said. I lowered my cup. "Did you put something in it to get revenge?" Roxlin asked Kaylon accusingly.

Kaylon raised his hands in a peaceful gesture. "Of course I didn't! I bet it tastes fine and you're just overreacting." Curious, I once again raised my cup and this time took a sip. Kaylon was right. It tasted fine to me.

However, it was weird. Though Roxlin was good at lying, she didn't do so for the fun of it. That gave me the option to decide between whether Kaylon was lying or if Roxlin was lying. I, of course, believed my cousin over the Alligator Lyven. But I kept quiet, interested to see where the situation was going. Kaylon hadn't lied to us before, as far as I could tell. So what would be his purpose for lying here?

Then it hit me.

Kaylon must have done what I'd ask him to do.

The Alligator Lyven gave Roxlin a sly grin. "I can take

your cup back if you're *too good* for the water being provided here."

Roxlin glared back and, after a moment's hesitation, she chugged the rest of the water without breaking eye-contact. "You were saying?" she shot back hotly.

Kaylon gave a genuine smile now. "Nothing. I was saying nothing." The Alligator Lyven shot me a meaningful look, confirming my suspicion. I closed my eyes and smiled.

The four of us talked for a little bit more until, suddenly, chaos broke out.

Screams from the far side of the room where the musicians had just stopped playing sounded around the beautiful dance hall. Roxlin and I tried to see what was going on, but a wave of Lyvens trying to escape whatever unseen horror that had appeared came crashing into us, pushing us along with the flow.

Separated from the rest of my group, I glanced frantically around, trying to find a place where I wouldn't be shoved by the panicked Lyvens. A place where I could find a way to get back to Roxlin.

I finally managed to break free of the throng, and found myself at the very edge of the dance floor. Searching the mass of bodies for my cousin didn't help; I wasn't tall enough or able to stand somewhere that gave me a good vantage point. But several familiar seven-foot tall creatures were lumbering in my direction from a hole they had smashed through the wall of the room.

I tried to turn and run to avoid the monstrous Corrupted so that I could get back to Roxlin, but I was frozen. Memories of the Corrupted from my past lives flickered through my brain, uncontrollable. Fear that the memories brought left me unable to think rationally, let alone move. I could only stand there as the six lumbering Corrupted ran towards me.

Pushing through the Lyvens who weren't able to get out of the way and consequently turning the poor victims into screaming hosts of the Corruption, they finally reached me.

I closed my eyes and sent a mental apology to Cillium. I was a failure. Unable to perform my duties unlike my lives before. I was, and would forever be known, as useless.

"Ari!" My eyes snapped open just in time to see Roxlin barrel into me. She pushed me out of the way of the Corrupted that had just been about to overtake me. And in doing so, the Corrupted crashed right into her.

"*NO!*" I screamed.

Chapter 18
Roxlin

I didn't think. All I knew was that I had to get Arizu out of the way of the Corrupted. So it ended up being that, after pushing her out of harm's way, I had no plan of getting *myself* out of danger.

Being slammed into by a Corrupted wasn't a pleasant feeling by all means. It was a seven-foot tall beast made of bubbling black goo, after all. As I went flying, I braced myself for what I assumed would be a painful process of being taken over by the Corruption. But when I landed and nothing happened after a few seconds, I sat up, confused. I felt pain in my left leg from my hard landing, but nothing else.

Glancing around, I saw Arizu staring at me with a look of horror and saw Kiara, Kaylon, Mina, and Feyor fighting back what had to be at least six Corrupted. Arizu didn't even seem to notice the extra company and ran to me as fast as she could.

She fell to her knees beside me when she reached where I sat. "Rox, you're okay, right? *Please* tell me you're okay."

I glanced over myself. "I guess so? I don't understand how, though."

Arizu pulled me into a hug. "It doesn't matter how. I'm just glad you're alright." Still confused, I pulled away from my cousin and watched the fight in front of me unfold. It may not matter to Arizu why I hadn't been corrupted, but I needed answers. It didn't make sense.

I glanced over at my cousin as she stood with a determined look on her face.

"I'm sorry," she told me as she watched the fight as well. "The words of the spell came back to me this morning, but I was selfish and still wanted to attend the ball. And now. . . My selfishness nearly cost you your life."

Arizu bent over and placed her hand on my shoulder. She looked me straight in the eyes, sincerity brimming in her own large, brown eyes. "Thank you," she said. "Thank you for being such a wonderful cousin, and such a wonderful friend. I probably wouldn't have lived as long as I did if you hadn't been there for me." Arizu's words just made me more confused.

"What are you talking about?" I asked her. "It sounds like you're about to go die or something." Arizu just smiled sadly at me and turned away. I grabbed her arm and tried to stand. Unfortunately, as I put weight on my injured left leg, it crumpled beneath me and, with a grunt, I fell to the ground once again. I kept a tight grip on Arizu's arm, however. There was no way I was letting her go without getting answers. "What's going on?" I asked her angrily.

The sincerity in my cousin's eyes turned to sadness. "Kiara finished another Corrupted vaccine and gave it to me yesterday. But when she left I. . . gave it to Kaylon. I told him that I didn't care how he did it, but to just get you to take it. So earlier, in your water. It had the vaccine in it. That was why it tasted weird." I released Arizu's arm in shock. My cousin backed away quickly so that I couldn't reach her anymore. Continuing, she said, "I'm sorry. I need to go now. I need to get to the Corruption's Gate."

"The Corruption's Gate?" I repeated. I didn't understand. "Ari, just tell me what's going on!"

Arizu shook her head. "Kaylon will keep you safe." My cousin began running towards the fight going on. She veered back towards the entrance of the ballroom when she almost reached the battling Lyvens.

"Mina!" She called. "Get me to the Corruption's Gate as fast as you can!" Mina immediately obeyed and broke away from the fight, shifting into a horse as she did so. Without either one breaking a stride, Arizu grabbed Mina's mane and swung herself onto the galloping Horse Lyven's back. I watched, helpless.

Without Mina's support, the Corrupted began pushing Feyor, Kiara, and Kaylon back. And it didn't help that the several unlucky victims that had been in the way of the monsters' rampage were now changed and coming to join.

When the battle had almost reached my position, Kiara called out, "Kaylon, take Roxlin and get her away from here! Feyor and I can keep these Corrupted distracted long enough for Arizu to finish this." Kaylon broke away without hesitation and scooped me up in his arms, bridal style. He ran the same route Mina and Arizu had taken. We exited the ballroom.

"Put me down," I demanded.

Kaylon gave me a confused look and kept running. "I'm not putting you down. I need to get you out of danger."

"Put me down, or I will bite your arm."

Kaylon hesitated, slowed, and then stopped. But he didn't put me down. "Why aren't you letting me take you to a safe place?" He gave me an angry look.

"Because I don't need you to take me to a safe place. I need you to take me to where Arizu is going. Take me to the Corruption's Gate, whatever that is, now."

Kaylon shook his head. "No. Not gonna happen."

"Kaylon," I said, desperation slipping into my voice. "My cousin, who is more like a sister to me, who is more my family than my own *parents*, just said what seemed like a final good-bye. And I didn't get to say anything back. *Please*, Kaylon. Please take me to Arizu."

Kaylon looked away for a moment, and then sighed. "Alright," he said. "But we won't catch them in time by taking the regular route." The Alligator Lyven began running once again. "Remember those secret passages throughout the palace that Mina told you about?" I nodded. "There are a few that lead right to the room you need to get to."

I smiled at Kaylon. "Thank you, Kaylon. Thank you so much." Kaylon just continued running.

To make it easier on the Alligator Lyven, I shifted to my snake form and wrapped myself around his neck. Before long, we came to an old tapestry that Kaylon pulled to the side. He quickly pressed a specific brick in, and a small door opened up. We went through while the door shut behind us.

The passage was smooth, square, and too small for

Kaylon to stand up straight. So, crouching, the Alligator Lyven proceeded through the twists and turns in confidence, small stones that gave off a soft glow lighting his way.

"Roxlin," Kaylon began as he made his way through the passage. "I wanted to let you know that Arizu no longer desires to be completely free from emotional pain like before. Her deepest desire now is to save Cillium and keep everyone safe. I hope. . . well. . . I hope this puts your mind at ease about her well-being even if just by a little bit. Even with whatever happens next." It didn't, but being in my snake form, I couldn't reply. I just hoped we got to the Corruption's Gate before anything else terrible happened.

After what seemed like an eternity, Kaylon finally stopped at what seemed like a dead end. "Behind this door is the Corruption's Gate," he said. "Are you prepared for what you might find?"

I steeled myself and shifted back to my humanoid form. "It doesn't matter if I am or not. I need to see my cousin again." Nodding once, Kaylon pressed one of the glowing stones to the right of the "dead end", and a hidden door slid to the side, revealing an almost completely empty chamber.

It was circular and bare of any ornaments. But in the center of the room was a blue/white light that looked almost identical to the Gate that connected Cillium to Earth. It was the only source of light in the otherwise dark room and could only be one thing: the Corruption's Gate.

Shadows covered the open space, and standing among those shadows were five figures. Three of the figures blocked the way to the Gate, and the other two, who I recognized immediately as Arizu and Mina, looked prepared to fight their way through.

"We have to go help them!" I said to Kaylon.

He shook his head. "*I* will go help them. *You* will stay here." Before I could object or react, Kaylon set me down gently and ran to stand beside his sister. Ignoring his words, I shifted forms and began slithering slowly towards the stand-off. Even as I hurried as fast as I could while fighting through the pain in my tail, I could tell the situation was escalating.

"Even with another Lyven to help, you don't stand a chance against us," a familiar voice hissed. I recognized my mother standing in the middle of who I could now see to be Selen, the Eagle Lyven, and Kren, the Leopard Lyven. The light from the Gate threw shade across their faces, making it hard to see their facial expressions.

"Selen," Arizu said in a calm voice. "When we first met, your words were sharper than a knife to almost everyone. But, besides stabbing me, you've shown no hostility towards me. I don't think you really want to do this. I think that, deep down, you know that what the Corruption has promised you will never come true."

"Don't speak, Selen," my mother ordered.

Despite her demand, Selen, conflict written across his face, replied, "My daughter died of a rare, incurable disease four years ago. The Corruption promised it could revive her. But you just. . . You look and act so much like her, Arizu. I. . . I just want my daughter back."

"Selen!" my mother warned with a dark look.

Ignoring her, Arizu said, "Selen. The Corruption is an evil thing. It can't bring your daughter back to life. But you can honor her memory by doing the right thing here. Stand down."

Kaylon now spoke. "The same applies to you, Kren," he said, addressing the Leopard Lyven.

Kren growled. "Shut up," he snarled. "I'm getting my wife back, no matter what." I finally made it next to where Arizu stood. I debated whether or not I should shift back to my humanoid form, but decided against it. I'd just be a sitting duck with my injured left leg.

"Enough of this!" my mother said, baring her fangs. "Let's end this once and for all, *half-breed mutt*." My mother charged at Arizu, and my cousin side-stepped, kicking the Snake Lyven in the back as she passed. Pulling a knife from somewhere on her person, Mother struck at Arizu's neck. My cousin ducked and jumped back out of reach. The two circled.

On the other side of Arizu, Kaylon fought Kren, both shifted to their animal forms, while Mina fought Selen. It was obvious, however, that Selen was dragging his feet. And I heard Mina give a final, gentle push on the Eagle Lyven.

"Help us, Selen. Don't you think that's what your daughter would have wanted?" she asked gently.

Selen slowed his movements, and then stopped. "You're right," he said. "She wouldn't want me to doom our entire race just because I was unwilling to let her spirit rest in peace." With that, he turned and tackled Kren as the Leopard Lyven was about to leap onto Kaylon's back. Shifting into his eagle form, he dove at Kren's eyes, keeping him at bay.

"Traitor!" Kren snarled.

Satisfied that Mina, Kaylon, and Selen would be able to

handle Kren, I turned my attention back to the fight between Arizu and my mother. Only, my mother had disappeared. In this shadowy of a room, she was able to use her ability to its highest extent. Jumping in and out of visibility, she slashed at Arizu's arms and legs, trying to maim her. Arizu managed to avoid most of her attacks, but slits of blood showed across my cousin's arms where my mother was able to land some blows.

Knowing the others were still too busy with Kren, I shifted back to my humanoid form and yelled, "Mother, stop!"

To my surprise, she did. Appearing from the shadows, she said, "Daughter. What are you doing here?"

"I came to see Arizu. And now I see you here attacking her? What could the Corruption have possibly promised you that would make you turn on your own kind? Your own *kin?*"

My mother stared me, coldness in her eyes. "It promised me Arizu's death. That's all it needed to do." My mother's words chilled me to the core. How could I have not seen the darkness inside of her throughout my entire life? She couldn't have always been like this, could she have? Saying nothing more, my mother disappeared.

"Stop hiding in the shadows," Arizu called out, inching her way towards me. Probably trying to protect me. But no matter what, my mother wouldn't hurt me. At least, that's what I had thought.

As I sat there, I felt cool metal press against my throat.

"Don't come any closer, *mutt*," my mother hissed as she held her knife against my throat. "Unless you want me to cut your precious cousin's throat open."

Arizu's eyes darkened. "You've made a grave mistake,

Viern," she said with a dangerous edge to her voice. "Once I enter the Corruption's Gate, everyone's memories concerning me and the Corruption will be erased, including yours. All you had to do was let me fulfill my duty, and everything would have gone back to the way it was. However, you've shown that you are beyond saving." Without breaking eye contact with my mother, she said only one word. "Selen."

I heard the *whoosh* of air, and then the knife that had been pressed against my skin fell away. I turned, dazed, and saw my mother stumble back, shock across her face. The hilt of a knife showed just above her left shoulder, angled down into her heart. Selen stood behind her in his humanoid form, a grim look on his face. With a final gasp, my mother fell to the ground.

My throat tightened and I could barely breathe as I crawled as quickly as I could to my mother's corpse. Yes, she had been harsh and cold, even willing to kill me at the end of her life. Even so, she had still been my mother.

I gathered her body into my arms and choked on the lump in my throat. A gentle presence next to me made me look up.

Arizu crouched beside me, compassion on her face. "I'm sorry it had to end this way," she said softly. "And I'm so sorry I can't be here to comfort you." She lowered her head. "I must go now."

"Wait!" I cried out as my cousin stood and turned towards the Gate. "Don't leave me alone. Please. Don't leave me, Ari."

Sadness flashed through Arizu's eyes as she looked at me. "To keep you safe, I must sacrifice myself for the spell to work. See, the spell I cast to trap the Corruption during my first life is dark magic. It takes human sacrifice to complete. And I would not sacrifice anyone else. Now, only my blood can act as the seal." Arizu stared at the shadows of the room. "In their study of *Blood Ties*, my mom and dad would have come across this information. They didn't only not want me to have to carry a burden of destiny, as King Rolm and Queen Aulia said. They were trying to save my life.

"But Rox, you aren't alone. The blood of my heritage ties me to this fate, yes. But you still have Mina, Kiara, your father, and especially Sou and Kaylon, who will always be by your side."

"But. . . will you really disappear from everyone's memories?" I managed to ask around the lump in my throat.

Arizu nodded. "That is how previous monarchs designed this world to be. King Rolm and Queen Aulia will remember everything, of course. As well as any future monarchs as this knowledge is passed to them. The King and Queen also know the formula for Kiara's vaccine. So, hopefully, next time I'm reborn and the Corruption comes back, we can defeat this thing once and for all." Arizu turned away and walked towards the Corruption's Gate. Though right before entering the blue/white light, she turned back around one last time. "Take care of Roxlin for me, Kaylon," she said. "She's a handful, but I'm sure you're ready for the task."

"It will be my pleasure," Kaylon said with a bow. Following suit, Mina and Selen bowed to Arizu in a respectful farewell.

Glancing at me for a final time, Arizu clasped her hands behind her back and gave me her trademark cheesy smile that I knew so well. I hadn't seen that smile since the meeting with the King and Queen. And it broke my heart.

"'Till we meet again, Roxlin," she said. Then saying words in a language I didn't know, she stepped backwards into the light. My cousin, my best friend, my *family*, vanished in an instant.

I wanted to cry, but my snake eyes wouldn't allow me to. I pulled my mother's body close to my chest and gritted my teeth, the lump in my throat making it hard to breathe. Gentle arms wrapped around me and held me as the air stilled, the only sound being the snuffling of an unconscious Kren.

"'Till we meet again, Arizu," I whispered into the silence.

After a few more moments, the Corruption's Gate faded away, and my mind went blank.

Twelve Years Later

I placed the final dish in the dishwasher as small feet pattered in my direction. I turned to meet my daughter as she raced into the kitchen.

"Mama!" she said in excitement. "Can I go play with Jyr?" She hopped up and down in anticipation of my answer.

I smiled fondly at my daughter and, kissing her head, said, "Of course, Arizu. Go have fun." With an excited squeal, Arizu ran outside.

Joining me as I looked out the window at our five-year-old daughter, Kaylon wrapped an arm around my shoulders and pulled me close to him.

"She's such a lively little thing, isn't she," he said with a smile. He then tilted his head in thought. "Doesn't she remind you of someone, though?"

I continued to stare out the window. "She does." Hazy memories flashed through my brain, seeming just out of grasp. "She reminds me of someone I was close to. I can't remember that Lyven very well, but I have a feeling it's because of her that we're able to have this life together."

Kaylon looked at me, love in his eyes. "Well, then I'm eternally grateful to that Lyven."

I smiled at my husband. "Me too."

The End